Return Of The Mountain Man

Tom Franklin traveled west to hunt and trap in the majestic Rocky Mountains until the need to protect his family threatened to surpass the lure of the high peaks.

James Oliver Virmala

Edition 2

Cover Photo By James Oliver Virmala

"Yellowstone"

ISBN: 978-0-9972536-6-5

ACKNOWLEDGMENTS

In WWII, three U.S. soldiers were lost behind enemy lines when the Germans made their push during the Battle of the Bulge. For three frigid days and nights, they hid within earshot of the Germans, huddling together for warmth.

The cold and hunger finally forced them to approach a Belgium farmhouse. They were fully aware that the farmer might turn them over to the Germans, but the freezing temperatures and lack of food made them risk knocking on the door.

They were greeted by a Belgian farmer, who provided them with food and a place to hide. He then guided them back to an American armored unit. For his own safety, the man left just short of the American line and returned to his farm. I owe a debt of gratitude to this unknown farmer, who led my father and his fellow soldiers out of German-held territory.

CONTENTS

BOOKS BY THE AUTHOR

Oli's Gold Book One
Search For Oli's Gold Book Two
Return To Oli's Gold Book Three
To Be A Mountain Man
Trouble On The Kansas Plains
Frontier Justice
Return Of The Mountain Man
The Tall Man
The Prospector
The Green Valley
Twilight Of The Mountain Man
The Mother Lode
Quest Of The Mountain Man
Journey's End
Rufus Pike
Rufus And The Pup
The Winding Trail Home
Rufus The Lost Years
The Kankakee Kid
Bogus Island
Tyler Tomas The Brothers' War
War of 1812 The Choice
Kyle Oliver The Next Horizon

CHAPTER ONE

The summer sun blazed down on the wide plain as a lone wagon slowly moved across the wheatgrass and sage-covered swells. They were near the end of their second hunt and the wagon was nearly loaded with buffalo hides harvested over the past two weeks. Buzzards rode the heat waves above, anticipating feeding on the carcasses left behind from the next stop.

A tall, broad-shouldered mountain man, Tom Franklin, rode alongside. The wagon was driven by a square-jawed man named Chess Handlin. Tom had first met Chess on the way to the Green River rendezvous. He had run into him again at the fort. With money being short, they'd decided to work together on a couple of summer hunts. They could then fund a winter of trapping on the Wind River Range.

Ahead of the wagon rode a white-haired Indian named Two Buffalo. He had been a Cheyenne chief at one time. He and the mountain man had met while Tom was on his first trapping expedition. Their friendship had prevented Two Buffalo from living his last days in his death lodge. Instead of starving to death, Tom had given the old chief a reason to live by mentoring the young trapper.

Tom's wife Eva, an Arapahoe, sat alongside Chess on the wagon. Her extended stomach was evidence that she would soon be giving birth. The mountain man had encouraged her to remain at Fort William, but she had insisted on being with him, assuring Tom that they would be back at the fort well before the baby came.

It was late July 1842. The buffalo were plentiful on the plain. Two Buffalo ranged ahead of the wagon, looking for good-sized herds to hunt and also to help avoid obstacles that could hamper the hide wagon.

The chief stopped his horse on a rise and pointed to the west. He had spotted a herd of buffalo grazing on the wheatgrass. Tom brought his animal to a trot and rode to his friend. Looking at the valley ahead, the mountain man smiled.

"It's a good herd," he acknowledged. "We'll set up camp and be ready to start shooting in the morning."

The old chief had a grave look on his face. "I have cut sign of riders for the past two days. They could be other tribes hunting buffalo, but we haven't found any remains of their kills."

Tom looked at the chief. "Between you and that mule, we'll have plenty of warning if they come around. Another two days of shooting and we'll have a load and head for the fort."

Two Buffalo was confident that he'd know if anyone came close. He also knew that Tom and Chess would be fearless in a fight, but he worried about Eva. He didn't doubt her nerve, knowing that she had survived being captured by Comancheros and had managed to escape and evade them until he and Tom found her. But now she was with child and would require protection if they were attacked, taking away from those fighting.

While Tom and Chess set up camp, Two Buffalo rode out onto the plain, searching for any new sign that could warn of what might be coming. The mountain man watched his friend ride away. He realized that the chief's warning had to be taken seriously, but money from the buffalo hides was needed.

While they set up the camp, Eva got a cook fire going using buffalo chips gathered while traveling. After a troop tent was erected and the gear stowed, the two men got their Hawken rifles out to ready them. Tom always had his Colt Paterson on his hip, except when skinning buffalo. Chess kept one of his single-shot handguns in his waist band.

The rifles were leaned against the wagon when they saw that Eva had the meal ready. She brought them two plates with sliced buffalo tongue and beans. Tom looked at her and a flash of worry crossed his face. She was looking tired.

"You should be resting more. We can fix our own supper," he told his wife.

"It is good for the baby if I keep busy," she assured him.

By the time the sun was low in the west, the herd of buffalo had moved about a mile from the camp. Once dark they would settle down for the night. Two Buffalo rode back into camp and sat down, taking the plate of food Eva had ready for him.

The three men sat near the fire, with Tom and Chess drinking the last of the coffee and Two Buffalo with a mug of tea. The men were planning the morning hunt. They would shoot 16 to 20 buffalo for skinning tomorrow and then move with the herd to shoot again the next day before heading back to the fort.

As darkness closed over the plain, the fire was allowed to burn down. Tom joined Eva, who had already gone to bed in the army tent. Chess slept under the open sky a short distance from the fire. Two Buffalo would make his bed near the picketed stock. The sounds of fox and wolves hunting floated across the plain. Grunts and snorts from some of the buffalo that passed close to the camp could be heard.

The morning chill greeted the man as they crawled out of their blankets. Chess and Tom were ready to start shooting at first light. Tom had left Eva sleeping, hoping she would get some extra rest. They led the mule that carried a pack containing items needed for shooting and skinning the buffalo, along with Tom's Colt Paterson ball and cap revolver, hanging from the packs. Walking out to take position for shooting, they chewed on hard bread. It was washed down with sips from their canteens.

The men stopped near some boulders about 100 paces from the herd. The buffalo were just starting to get up, with many of them rolling to coat their hides with dust to protect them against flies and parasites.

While Chess picketed the mule, Tom laid out packets of powder, oiled patches, and lead balls on the flat top of one of the boulders. He also placed the loaded Colt on the boulder. The high desert air was still cool and they could feel it through their woolen shirts. With everything ready, they both took a chew of tobacco and sat watching the herd. Soon the buffalo would spread out grazing, and then it would be time to shoot.

Eva was lying in the tent when she heard the first shot. She had intended to get up early enough to make coffee for the men before they went out to shoot. She had been in a half-sleep when Tom had gotten up. Eva had spent much of the night trying to get comfortable and the baby had been kicking.

She sat up and placed her hand on her stomach. "You just be patient, little one. We'll be back in Fort William in a week and then you can show yourself." Her breasts were swollen with milk and she knew it would be soon.

When she was younger, Eva had witnessed many babies being born while the tribe was traveling from one hunting ground to another. The birth was taken in stride, with the mother often continuing the trip while giving the child its first milk. Now she sat listening to the methodical firing of the rifles, and counting the number of kills.

Near the herd, Tom placed the cap on the nipple of his Hawken and took aim at the last animal for the mornings shooting. A large bull was sniffing at one of the buffalos that they had shot previously. Lining his sights on the shoulder of the wooly beast, he pressed the set trigger. As he slowly exhaled, Tom squeezed the hair trigger and the Hawken recoiled sending a killing ball at the animal. On impact, its head came up suddenly and then it turned to start running before collapsing onto the grassy plain.

The two men loaded their rifles once more before putting the packs back on Ralph. They had two makeshift scabbards to slide the Hawken's into. They led the mule toward two downed buffalo that were furthest from the herd. Tom dropped the mules lead rope, knowing it would stay nearby while they did the skinning. Both men took their whetstones and honed the skinning knives before beginning the work of removing the hides.

It began with a slit from chin to tail and up the legs. Then they gripped the hide, tearing it back while loosening it from the carcass with their knives. Completing the task on one side, they used the legs to roll the animal over to begin on the other side. Both men took advantage of a rope fastened to the sawbuck on the mule to maneuver the buffalo and haul the carcass off the skinned hide.

Each carcass had enough meat to feed four people for over a month. The tribes would use the bones to make arrowheads, knives, clubs, pipes, and other tools. All Tom and Chess were taking were the hides. The meat was left to rot and be torn at by wildlife on the plain. While the men didn't realize it now, in years to come after many thousands of buffalo had been killed for their hides, the bones left behind would have value and be harvested for carbon to refine sugar and to make fertilizer.

They had shot 18 buffalo in less than 30 minutes. Working straight through, it would take four hours to skin the animals, then another four hours to scrape the hides and spread them out for drying. The buzzing of flies was loud as they were attracted to the carcasses. The buzzards stood in clusters a short distance away, waiting. Flashes of wolves could be seen as they moved ever closer.

Suddenly, Tom caught another movement to

his right. It was Eva coming to get some meat. When they had camped in one place for several days, she would cut the tender loins to make jerky. Today it was just for their supper and when she had the meat she wanted, Eva waved at the two men and headed back to the camp. Tom shook his head. She was moving slowly now and should be resting. She was a strong-willed woman, and while that was one of the things the mountain man loved, it created some frustration.

When they got to the final couple of animals, Two Buffalo came down with the team horses, which he'd put sawbuck saddles on. The folded hides lay near the buffalos that had been skinned and he piled them onto the horses and brought them to the camp. By the time the last buffalo was skinned, he was ready for the hides.

Tom and Chess cleaned their hands as best they could on the wheatgrass and then followed the chief back to camp, leading Ralph and touching up the knives with their whetstones on the way. Eva had the Dutch oven filled with warm water so the men could wash up a bit. She had fried buffalo along with some of yesterday's beans, and fresh coffee for them.

She sat next to Tom while he ate. He noticed that she was losing color. "I want you to rest while we scrape the hides," he told her.

"I can spread them out for you and have them ready to hang on the poles," Eva replied.

Tom placed his hand on her stomach and felt the baby kick. "The little one in there agrees with me," he said. "If you don't rest, the baby will be wanting out to see what's going on."

Despite her objections, Tom was able to convince her to rest while they took care of the hides.

He did notice that she put on more coffee for them before going to the tent. Both ends were tied open to allow the breeze to blow through. As Tom and Chess began the chore of processing the hides, Two Buffalo walked from the camp with his Kentucky Long Rifle cradled in the crook of his arm, watching the plain around the camp.

The incessant buzzing of flies and the foul smell of the wagon in the hot sun was a constant companion of the hunters. The green hides left a scent clinging to them that would take a lot of future washing to remove. As the two men scraped meat and fat from the hides, their buckskin clothes were covered with grease and blood as well as the tall sides of the wagon.

Unknown to the sweat-covered men, there were three Crow braves lying hidden in the needle and wheatgrass, east of the camp, just over a rise. The braves were observing the buffalo hunters as they worked on the hides. A lean brave with a scar across his left cheek squinted as he watched. His focus was on the tent as well as Tom and Chess.

The two loaded rifles leaned against the wheel of the hide wagon, within easy reach. The 16-inch skinning knives flashed as they worked on hides hanging from pole frames. Two Buffalo stopped near the working hunters and stared in the direction of the Crow.

"I feel we are being watched," he said. "I can smell the stink of Crow. They hide in the grass like cowardly mice."

Tom looked at his Colt Paterson hanging on the tailgate of the wagon, wondering if he should put it on. He glanced at the few hides they had left to process and decided to wait until they were done.

"We don't need Indian trouble now," he said, searching the plain in the direction that the old man was watching. Tom then looked at the tent where Eva was resting.

Two Buffalo moved away from the camp, staring to the east. Feeling uncomfortable with the piercing, searching eyes of the old man, the Crow carefully worked their way away from the buffalo hunters. Once below the rise, they quickly put distance between themselves and the camp.

Worry filled the broad-shouldered mountain man as he continued to work under the hot sun. His curly, brown hair sticking out from the bottom of his flat-brimmed hat was plastered to his forehead. He was worrying about the woman in the tent that he'd married just a year ago, at Fort William.

Finishing the last hide, Tom stood and stretched to take the kinks out of his back. "Two Buffalo thinks some braves are looking over our camp," he told his friend. "With today's hunt we should be close to a full wagon of hides."

Chess looked up from his work and sat back on his heels. Honing his knife on the whetstone, he said, "Another day or two and we can head for the fort. Your mule and Two Buffalo will keep an eye out for any trouble."

Putting the stone into his possible bag, he added, "It will be good to get away from the smell of rotting carcasses and the hide wagon."

"I believe much of the smell is on us," Tom said, chuckling. He looked up at the cottony clouds in the sky. "Let's spread today's hides on the grass and let them dry for a couple hours before dark."

After arranging the hides, the two men cleaned

up as best they could with the water remaining in the Dutch oven and then poured themselves mugs of coffee. It was strong and black, having been near the fire since earlier that day.

Tom was anxious to finish the hunt and get back to Fort William. There was a midwife who could assist with the birth of their child, and he said so to Chess.

Two Buffalo came over, chewing on a piece of jerky. "We are being watched," he said with certainty. "For two days I have cut sign and smelled them. Tomorrow, we should end the hunt and go back to the fort. Today there were only a few. Soon, more will come and there will be trouble."

Chess and Tom looked at each other and nodded. "The trip back will take less than a week," Chess said. "We have enough hides already between the two hunts. We should leave first thing in the morning."

"It is set then," Tom agreed. "We will make the wagon ready to move first thing in the morning. Two Buffalo, you let us know if they come back."

On the hunts the old Indian chief had been responsible for guarding the camp. He did this with the help of the mule, Ralph, who would alert them of intruders during the night. Other than their weapons and scalps, marauding Indians would be after their stock. Chess rode a buckskin, Two Buffalo a paint, Tom a dun and there were two bays that pulled the wagon.

If they were attacked and the Crow were successful, that would leave his pregnant wife. Tom was almost made ill by his last thought. It would be better if they all died, rather than Eva to remain alive and at their mercy.

"These are stupid thoughts!" the mountain man hissed, scolding himself.

Tom and Chess were cleaning their Hawkens near the fire when Two Buffalo brought his long rifle to them. "I will be back before daylight," he told them and disappeared into the dark with his bow and knife.

That night, Tom found sleeping difficult. His mind was racing as he worried about the woman lying beside him. When he did doze, he was awakened by dreams of hostiles appearing out of the dark. The wind was whipping the wheatgrass and tearing at the canvas tent when Tom gave up trying to sleep. He pulled the Colt and holster out from under his saddle.

It was still dark when he crawled out. He sat for a moment as he looked around their camp before strapping the revolver to his hip. He could see the still form of Chess sleeping with his blankets over his head. After pulling his boots on, he stood with his hand on his Colt. He walked over to check on the horses and mule.

The animals stood staring to the east of the camp. There was something, or someone, coming from that direction. Tom crouched, searching the darkness. Out of the night came the sound of a dove. Cupping a hand to his mouth, he cooed a response. A couple of minutes later, the dark form of Two Buffalo appeared.

"I thought I should warn you I was coming so you wouldn't shoot me," Two Buffalo said.

"It was a wise thing to do," Tom admitted. "Even knowing our signal, it was still a worry."

"They're camped an hour to the north," the old man said.

"How many?" Tom asked.

"I counted six. There were no women or children with them."

Tom stood watching his old friend and waited. He was sure that there was more to tell.

"I had to take care of the one watching the horses. I led their animals away and released them east of here. It should take them some time rounding them back up."

"Do you think they were hunting buffalo?" the tall man inquired.

"The horses had scalps hanging from their manes. Some of them from white men, some from other tribes. I am sure they planned to add ours to them," Two Buffalo said.

Tom could see the first light showing in the east. "You have given us maybe a day until they find the horses. I will get the others up, we have to leave now."

He turned and saw Chess sitting up, pulling on his boots. The cold wind was whipping up dust from the grass-covered plain. Before Tom got to the tent, Eva appeared through the flap.

He told them what Two Buffalo had found. In less than an hour, the camp was broken down and they were on the move back toward the fort.

Chewing on a piece of jerky as he drove the wagon, Tom had his eyes on the horizon. His dun was tied with the mule to the back of the wagon. The mule carried a pack with their gear and supplies. Eva sat next to him, working on a cradleboard for their baby. Chess rode his buckskin ahead, scouting out the best route for the heavily loaded wagon.

Two Buffalo followed behind the wagon, at

times as much as a mile from them. He spent much of his time watching their back trail, looking for any pursuit. He trusted that his paint could quickly close the gap between himself and the wagon if he saw danger.

The team strained under their load as the wagon moved through a sandy area. The wind created swirling spirals of dust and sand that would sweep past the wagon, leaving the riders covered with the stinging dirt.

They stopped at a stream lined with cottonwood for a brief midday break. Eva dug out some stale sourdough biscuits and jerky for them, with water to drink. The trees gave them some break from the wind.

Tom would have loved to make some coffee, but they didn't dare take the additional time. He used a piece of rag to wipe the dust from the horses' noses. They were watered and given the last of the grain. The water barrel strapped to the hide wagon was refilled.

Chess watched for trouble with Two Buffalo, while Tom readied the team to continue. As the wagon pulled away from the cottonwood grove, the wind once again blasted them with dust and sand.

By mid-afternoon, they had to use their bandanas to cover their faces. Two Buffalo was somewhere behind them but, due to the dust, they were unable to see if he was near. Chess rode beside the wagon team, offering them some windbreak with his horse.

The sun had an eerie halo around it from the dust in the air. If the wind picked up anymore, Tom knew that they would have to pull up and sit out the storm. He was worried about Two Buffalo. He had not been seen since before their midday stop.

The struggling team began to falter by late afternoon. Tom knew that it was time to stop or risk losing horses. He decided that the next morning, if they could travel, he would use the dun and mule to pull the wagon and give the bays a rest.

They had to stop on open ground, at the mercy of the storm. While Chess took care of the stock, Tom used two of the hides and fashioned a windbreak across the bottom of the wagon.

Sitting against the hide-covered wagon, the three of them chewed on gritty jerky and sipped water. Tom looked out into the storm and wondered where Two Buffalo was. Had he been overtaken by the Crow, or could he have had an accident?

Chess decided to make their night quarters a little more secure by taking two of the poles used for hanging the hides and leaning them against the wagon. He then dragged a large hide off the wagon and hung it over the poles, giving cover from above. He staked the corners of the hide to the ground to prevent it from being blown off.

The hide wall buffeted them as the gusts of wind hit it. They used the pack of supplies from the mule to fashion a makeshift wall on one opening of their shelter. Darkness came early due to the dust blotting out the sun.

Tom sat with his arm around Eva when he felt her suddenly tense. If she made any noise, he did not know it due to the howling of the wind around them.

He held her close and asked, "What is it, Eva?"

"The baby," she gasped. "I think the baby is coming." Again, he felt her react to the pain.

For a desperate moment Tom prayed that the

labor would stop and they could get back to the fort before the baby was born. When she told him that her water had broken, he knew the birth would be tonight.

Tom shouted over the wind to Chess, "The baby is coming! Can you dig out a lantern and try and light it?"

In the near darkness, the soon-to-be-father attempted to make his wife comfortable. She grabbed his shirt sleeves and pulled him close to her. "You must help me, Tom. We can . . ." Releasing him, her body reacted to another pain.

Chess searched frantically for items to light the candle lantern. They usually did it with a twig lit from the camp fire. He had a flint and steel. In the cramped quarters with the wind and dust swirling, building a fire would be difficult.

Using his skinning knife, Chess cut a strip of cloth from his long johns. He rubbed it vigorously against his buckskin pants. Then, taking a bit of gun powder, he rubbed it into the greasy cloth.

He gathered some dry grass from just outside the opening and a tumble weed that had blown into their shelter. Digging a depression near the opening, Chess put in the cloth and grass. He then broke the tumble weed into pieces.

Straining his eyes, Chess looked in the direction of Tom and Eva. Their shadowy movements offered little evidence of what was happening. The howling wind masked any sounds.

Chess crawled out of the crude shelter and retrieved a bag of wooden stakes from the wagon. The blood and fat-covered stakes were used to secure the hides for scraping and drying. Ducking back into the shelter, Chess sat sneezing and coughing from the dust that coated his nostrils and throat.

Taking a moment to catch his breath, Chess used the skinning knife to cut slivers of wood for kindling. Then, taking several of the stakes, he piled them onto the tinder. With the wind and dust buffeting him, he moved outside the shelter, attempting to protect the fire pit with his body.

Chess felt for the pierced tin lantern to make sure that it was within reach. Then he struck the flint against the steel, sending a shower of sparks. The feeble light offered by the flint revealed that the gunpowder-covered cloth was buried under the stakes and tinder.

He felt his way through until his fingers touched the cloth. Keeping his hand close to it, he struck the flint on the steel. This time the shower of sparks was joined by a flash of ignited gunpowder. Chess jerked back his hand, shaking it as the burning powder burnt his fingers.

Soon, the tinder caught the fat-covered stakes on fire. In the flickering light of the fire he could now see Tom kneeling over Eva, trying to prepare her for the birth.

Using a splinter of wood, he tried to light the lamp. It took several tries before the wood stayed lit long enough in the wind to catch the candle wick on fire. Closing the hinged door, it offered a little more light than the fire.

Setting the lantern near Tom, Chess took the Dutch oven from the supply pack. Dumping his canteen into the oven, he replaced the cover and set it over part of the fire. The hardwood stakes would burn for a while and heat the water.

Moving next to Tom, he noticed that Eva's

doeskin dress was pulled up above her swollen stomach. Chess looked away, embarrassed by what he saw.

"I should probably go outside now," he told the expectant father.

"The hell you will, Chess!" Tom shouted over the wind. "I am just guessing here. I need all the help you can give me."

"What do you want me to do?" Chess shouted.

Without looking up, Tom replied in a hoarse voice, "Hold her head, wipe the dust from her face, and let Eva know you're nearby."

While the wind ripped at the green buffalo hides that made up their shelter, the two men helped the expectant mother as she struggled to bring new life into the violent frontier.

It was hours later when the cries of a new infant rose above the savage storm, demanding its voice in an unsure world. The lamp flickered on the two men, who had just witnessed the miracle of birth. Chess dug a shirt from their pack, tore off a sleeve and dunked it into the warm water in the Dutch oven. He handed it to Tom to clean the baby. A skinning knife was used to cut the cord before he began to wash his new son. Eva struggled to sit up and take her baby. Tom wrapped the newborn in the shirt Chess had gotten the sleeve off of and handed their son to his mother.

CHAPTER TWO

The only one who slept that night was the baby. Once the newborn was fed, he slept in his mother's arms, wrapped in the shirt. Shortly after the baby was born, the wind storm had dissipated.

Chess went out to check on the mule and horses. Tom used the rest of the hardwood stakes and kept the fire going. He roasted and crushed coffee beans and made a strong pot of the black brew. For Eva, Tom boiled some jerky to make a broth.

The sunrise was flaming red from the dust still hanging in the air. Chess was on watch. He saw movement along their back trail. With his Hawken at the ready, Chess was thankful when he recognized the rider as Two Buffalo.

The dust-covered chief dismounted from the paint and leaned against the horse for a moment before walking over to the wagon.

"We were worried about you," Chess said. He handed Two Buffalo his half-filled cup of coffee, then went to take care of the paint.

Tom came out of the makeshift shelter. "Two Buffalo, my friend! We have a baby!"

He then noticed that the chief was ready to collapse from exhaustion. Hurrying forward, he helped Two Buffalo to the fire. The old Indian sat against the wagon wheel and took a drink of the coffee, making a face from the bitter brew.

He looked up at Tom. "It is a son?"

"Yes, it is. His name is Isaac, after my brother," the tall man proudly said.

"I had a vision while in the storm. Your son will grow tall and strong like his father." Lowering the cup to his lap, the white-haired man closed his eyes and rested a moment before continuing.

"The Crow are camped a half-hour from here. They are now more than twelve. They will come soon," Two Buffalo said. "I found them yesterday and watched while they made medicine to prepare for the raid against us. They followed our wagon tracks until the storm stopped them."

"While they slept, I killed some of their horses with my bow under the cover of the storm. They will see the Cheyenne arrows. The Crow and Cheyenne have been enemies for a long time. They will have to make stronger medicine against a second enemy before they will be ready to come after us."

Two Buffalo held out his cup for more coffee. Tom watched his friend take a drink before saying, "With fewer horses, they will not be as fast, but they will come."

Chess came back from unsaddling the paint. Tom brought him up-to-date with what Two Buffalo had told him.

Chess looked at the heaping load of skins on

the wagon. "We can't outrun them with the wagon."

Nodding, Tom said, "There are too many of them to fight."

The two men looked at each other and knew what had to be done. All but a few of the hides had to be abandoned. The last several weeks of work was not worth dying for. With the lighter wagon they could make the fort in two days. Just maybe the Crow would find the hides and figure that it was enough of a victory and forget about chasing them.

Tom and Two Buffalo went to get the horses and mule. Chess had most of the hides unloaded when they got back to the wagon. Eva had the baby safely snuggled in the cradleboard.

"That should be enough, Chess," Tom called out. "Let's get the harnesses on the animals."

Chess told Tom that his horse had been used to pull a wagon before. The mule and buckskin were hitched to the wagon. The dun was saddled for Chess to ride. He would lead the paint while the two bays were tied to the back of the wagon.

The sun had not been up for an hour when they rode away in the wagon. Tom and Two Buffalo sat in the wagon seat and Eva and the baby rode in the back of the wagon, sitting on the remaining hides. The supply pack was near the back. The mountain man glanced back at his family and was thankful the sides of the hide wagon were higher than a farm wagon, giving more protection to them in case the Crow caught up.

The horses were kept at a mile eating trot. All three men carried their rifles at the ready. Chess also carried two single-shot pistols in his waistband. A .60 caliber, smooth-bore Mackinaw gun was in the wagon bed with Eva.

If they got into a running fight with the Crow, Tom would use the Mackinaw long gun to kill the braves' horses if they got close. It could be loaded and fired twice a minute. By using fine powder, a measure would be poured into the barrel. A tap of the stock put enough powder through the touch hole into the flash pan.

He would keep the bullets in his mouth. Then, dropping a ball into the bore, it would roll to the bottom, sticking to some of the powder. He would then aim and fire the weapon at the largest, close range target available. The large caliber bullet would kill horse or rider if they were hit.

Tom would depend on Eva to load his Hawken and Two Buffalo's Kentucky long rifle. These he would use when the Crow first came into range.

They stopped near a small brook to water and switch teams. With the bays back in the harness, they continued toward the fort. The lathered buckskin and mule were tied to the back of the wagon. Chess had switched to the paint.

Tom knew that the pace could kill the animals. The mule he called Ralph had been with him since he'd gone on his first buffalo hunt. It had faithfully carried him when he'd gone to save Eva from the Comancheros. Now, with danger following them, he had no choice but to push the animals.

Driving the wagon, Tom was tossed around by the rough ground. He looked back at Eva. She was nursing the baby. Her face was pale and he worried about the toll that this race for the fort would take on her.

Concentrating on the ground ahead of him, he

urged the tired horses to keep on. A shout from Eva alerted him to the pursuing Indians. They had split into two groups. They were closing in on both sides, riding on an angle that would intercept the wagon.

Tom shouted to Chess, "Come alongside and get in the wagon. You can fight from there!"

Chess rode next to the wagon and tossed his rifle into the bed. He then swung from the running paint and grabbed onto the side of the wagon, pulling himself over the edge and tumbled into the box. The dun and paint continued to run next to the wagon.

"Cut Ralph and the buckskin loose!" Tom yelled.

Without hesitation, Chess cut the animals free. While the mule continued to run with the fleeing wagon, the buckskin ran a few steps and came to a stop.

Most of the Crow carried bows. Those with long guns would have to stop to reload. Those firing arrows could be devastating at close range. The shrill cries of the attacking warriors were growing loud in the hunters' ears.

The attacking Crow braves were still out of rifle range. Tom handed the reins to Two Buffalo and climbed into the back of the wagon with Chess. Eva lashed the cradleboard with little Isaac to the side of the wagon.

As he pushed the tiring team, the white-haired chief moved his long rifle and bow within easy reach. Ahead he could see what might be a dry wash. Two Buffalo realized that the wagon would slow to a crawl crossing the boulder-strewn depression.

"It is a trap!" Two Buffalo shouted. "They plan to hit us at the wash ahead."

Slowing the wagon, he turned the team in the direction of the braves on the right. Rather than run, he was taking the fight to them!

Tom estimated that there were nine braves in front of him. He picked up some of the bullets for the Mackinaw gun. His mouth was dry and he feared that he would not have enough spit to wet them.

The distance between them and the attacking Crow closed quickly. Tom put his Hawken to his shoulder, picked out the running horse of one of the braves and fired.

The bouncing wagon made his shot go wide. Chess squeezed off a shot at the Crow. One of the horses stumbled and dumped its rider. Within moments, the wagon was among the charging Indians. The unexpected maneuver of driving at them rather than fleeing their attack caused confusion among the braves.

Tom was firing the Kentucky long rifle and his Hawken as fast as Eva could load them. Chess picked up the Mackinaw gun and loaded it, getting the saliva covered bullet from Tom. He pointed the weapon at a passing Indian horse and fired. He then drew his pistols and fired.

Tom emptied his Colt Paterson .36 caliber revolver at the painted bronze bodies of the attacking braves. Two Buffalo stood on the seat and fired arrows into the charging mass. With dust and clods of dirt flying around the wagon, the hunters broke free of the charging warriors.

Eva had the rifles loaded and the two men in the wagon box emptied them at the Crow horses. Tom could see that the second wave of braves would soon be within range. Two Buffalo kept the wagon running parallel to the wash.

Blood was running down the chief's arm as he slapped the team with the reins. He knew that one of the bays was hurt. It was lagging the other and would go down soon. The wagon was slowing, leaving them at the mercy of the Crow.

The bay on the right stumbled and went down. The wagon lurched to a stop. Two Buffalo climbed into the box with the other defenders.

The Crow moved away, outside of rifle range, and appeared to be planning their strategy for continuing the attack on the wagon. Tom climbed out, unhitched the remaining bay and tied it to the back of the wagon. If necessary, he hoped to send Eva and the baby out of danger while they held back the Crow.

Eva bandaged Two Buffalo's arm. Chess had a wound across the top of his shoulder and had packed a bandage under his shirt.

Climbing back into the wagon, Tom loaded the spare cylinders for his Colt. He looked over at Two Buffalo. "Why did they stop their attack?"

The old chief looked across the plain. "The area around us is open. The dry wash is 200 paces to the north. It offers little cover. During our first meeting we hurt them more than we were hurt. They know time is on their side. When they want to finish us, they will come."

While listening, Chess was loosening the water barrel and putting it inside the wagon. "We may be here for some time. At least we'll have water for a couple days," he said.

The sun blazed down on the wagon as the afternoon dragged on. The Crow numbers had decreased. Half of the remaining braves were gone.

Even though Tom and Chess were watching them, they did not see them leave.

Eva moved next to Tom. She had the baby in her arms. The new father looked at his family and felt tightness in his throat. There was a good chance that they would all be dead by this time tomorrow, and it was his fault that his wife and child were with them.

Chess had suggested leaving her at the fort. Eva had insisted on going and Tom had finally said she could. Even Two Buffalo had warned him of the dangers. Tom had let his weakness to please her make the decision rather than his head.

Eva moved to feed the baby and the men watched over the wagon sides at the Crow braves. Two Buffalo broke the silence. "They will come at us from the wash."

Tom glanced toward the boulder-strewn depression. "They would be dead before the distance could be covered."

"We will be looking in the wrong direction. The Crow that we can see will attack on a wide front. While we defend against them, the ones crawling up the wash will have no trouble closing in on us," Two Buffalo said.

The old chief took his knife. He looked at Tom and Chess. "I am going into the wash and wait for them. I may be able to break the charge and leave you to defend the south. I ask only one thing."

"What's that?" Chess asked.

"If you fire toward the wash, shoot the Crow, not me."

The chief dropped to the ground. Then, using the wagon and downed horse for cover, he made his way to the wash. Tom would have guessed that there was no place to hide in the shallow depression, but soon Two Buffalo disappeared from view.

Watching the spot where he last saw the chief, Tom said, "Goodbye, my friend. We will meet again on the other side."

He felt Eva's hand on his arm. Avoiding her eyes, he reached across and held her hand. *It's my fault, my fault*, he thought.

Tom knew that now wasn't the time for emotions. They had to be forced down inside. He had to concentrate on the fight that was coming. Adjusting his dark, flat-brimmed hat, he raised up to peer over the blood and fat-covered sides of the wagon.

There was a hissing sound and his hat was jerked off his head. An unseen brave had shot an arrow at him as he looked over the side. There was a severe burning on the top of his head where he had been clipped. The painted face of a Crow appeared over the south edge of the wagon, his arm raised while clutching a knife.

Tom instinctively raised the Colt and put a .36 caliber bullet between the fierce brown eyes. "Here they come!" he heard Chess shout. He looked up in time to see Chess use the butt of his Hawken to bash the head of another brave trying to get into the wagon.

Under their very noses, these Crow had crawled up to the wagon without being seen. They had initiated the attack. Alarm surged in Tom. His first instinct was to duck behind the wagon sides, but knew that he had a family and a friend depending on him to do his part.

Quickly checking that he had the extra Colt cylinders with him, he clutched the revolver and shouted to Chess, "I am going over to fight from under the wagon. Eva will load for you!"

Rolling out of the wagon on the wash side, he dropped to the ground. He anticipated seeing braves attacking from the wash. There were none. Scrambling under the wagon, he saw the bodies of the Crow who had tried to get into the wagon. He looked toward the mounted Indians.

They had spread out and were riding hard toward the wagon. Their shrill cries cut through the afternoon quiet. Tom's eyes went wide as another brave rose up 20 paces from the wagon and, keeping low, ran hard toward them.

He fired the Colt twice, spinning the running brave around. The Crow staggered a few more steps and fell. Tom could hear Chess firing above him. He lay under the wagon, waiting for the charging Indians to get within range of the Colt Paterson.

Suddenly, there were running footsteps behind him. They were coming from the wash! Tom turned, bringing the Colt to bear. It was Two Buffalo! Sliding into the dust beside him, the old chief peered at the Crow.

"You fire from here. I will help Chess in the wagon." As quickly as he had appeared beside Tom, Two Buffalo was gone and was shooting at the charging Crow from the wagon. Unable to hold his fire any longer, Tom emptied the Colt at the attackers.

Switching to a full cylinder, he looked at the warriors. Sudden calmness washed over him. Tom didn't know if he had accepted his fate of dying this day, or if it was knowing that he was part of a team fighting for survival. He moved to the front of the wagon and, kneeling behind the downed horse, systematically fired the Colt at the Indians.

Above him he heard the Hawken and long gun firing. As the Crow closed in there was also the distinctive sound of the Mackinaw gun. Several horses and braves lay wounded or dead on the grassy plain. The Crow thundered by the wagon.

Tom aimed the Colt at a fierce, painted brave with a scar on the left cheek. Swinging the revolver to keep it on his target, he squeezed the trigger. The hammer fell on an empty chamber.

Then the Crow were gone, riding hard away from them. Their cries could still be heard over the pounding of their horses' hooves. Looking around quickly, Tom could see no other targets. He was worried about his family and the others in the wagon.

"Is everyone okay in the wagon?" he hollered.

Getting no reply, he climbed up the front of the wagon. Two Buffalo sat watching for the return of the Crow. Eva was working on Chess, who was lying on the floor of the wagon.

"How bad is Chess hurt?" he asked.

Eva turned to her husband and then screamed, "Tom! You've been scalped!"

Tom had not realized that when his scalp had been creased, it had continued to bleed freely and the side of his head was covered with blood.

Dropping into the wagon, he knelt to check on his partner. "No, not scalped, just a cut on the top of my head," he assured Eva. Then he repeated, "How's Chess?"

"He was shot by a brave with a scar on his face. The bullet went through his arm and side," she said, struggling to tighten the crude bandage. "I think I've stopped the bleeding."

Tom moved next to her to check on his

wounded partner. She threw her arms around Tom and began to cry. As though feeling the distress of his mother, little Isaac began to cry, also.

For the next two hours, the occupants of the wagon watched for the return of the Crow. Tom helped Eva make Chess more comfortable against their supply pack. The sun was low in the west. It would be dark shortly.

"We need to move the dead away from the wagon," Two Buffalo cautioned. "The others will be back for the bodies."

Chess tried to sit up. "I can help move them." A wave of dizziness washed over him and he lay back heavily.

"You stay in the wagon," Tom warned. "You lost a lot of blood and moving around will get the wound bleeding again."

The bay was still tied to the back of the wagon. Tom used it to carry the bodies of the dead Crow away. He laid the dead braves alongside each other and folded their hands over their stomachs.

"The scalps are worth money," Two Buffalo reminded Tom.

"Yes, the folks overseas will pay good money for them," Tom agreed. "I think we will leave their topknots where they are."

Walking back toward the wagon, Two Buffalo caught an exhausted Crow pony that was standing with its head hanging low and tied it to the wheel. Eva had some supplies out and had lit a fire of buffalo chips.

The tired group sat chewing on jerky and drinking coffee. Some broth was made for Chess. Eva climbed into the wagon and helped him drink it. Chess was unable to stay awake, so she gave up and climbed back down and sat with Tom. The baby slept in his cradleboard next to his mother. Out on the plain, in the waning light, they could make out the carcasses of the dead Crow horses and the bodies of the slain braves.

Two Buffalo told them about the Crow in the wash. "After I found a place to hide, I waited. They came from up the wash. I could hear their bodies or clothing scrape against the ground. I worked my way around behind them."

"There were four young braves. Their eyes saw only to the front. They were looking forward to counting coup on us. They forgot to watch around them. From the back I crawled up and killed them one at a time. The last one turned a moment before I got to him and barely got out a word of his death song before I sent him to the other side."

Tom watched his old friend as he recounted the events in the wash. The white-haired chief's face was without expression except for a bit of sadness in his wise eyes. At a loss for words that would bring a smile to the sad eyes, he left his friend and went to take care of the horses.

As darkness settled around them, sand was thrown over the fire. Two Buffalo took the Crow pony and his bow. "I don't believe the Crow will be back. They will feel their medicine was too weak. I will be back before the first light."

Tom watched as his friend rode off into the night. He knew that the dead warriors would be gone by daybreak. Two Buffalo would be watching in the darkness, making sure that none of the Crow would be tempted to venture too close to the wagon.

Moving away from the wagon, Tom kept watch, looking into the darkness and listening for any sound that would warn him of another attack. While fighting to stay awake, the sound of Isaac's soft cry reached his ears. He heard Eva making ready to nurse the baby.

Pride surged through him as he thought about his new family. He vowed to do whatever he could to make sure that they were not put into any more danger. When he went to the Wind River to trap, he would find a safe place for Eva and the baby to winter.

Sometime before first light, Tom lost his struggle against sleep and dozed off. The feel of a hand on his shoulder woke him with a start. Swinging his rifle toward the intruder, he looked into the eyes of his wife.

Putting the Hawken down immediately, he apologized. "I'm sorry Eva, I must have fallen asleep."

"You needed the rest, husband. I have been watching for you," she said.

Eva went to check on Chess while Tom started putting together a small fire to make breakfast. His eye caught movement toward the east. In the early morning light, he saw a lone rider leading three horses. It was Two Buffalo returning. He was riding his paint and leading the buckskin, the dun, and the Crow pony.

CHAPTER THREE

The chief rode tall in the saddle as Tom took the extra animals from him. "They have left riding to the northwest," Two Buffalo told the mountain man as he slid off the paint.

"Do you think they will swing back east and be waiting for us?" Tom asked, concern on his face.

"They have too many dead," his friend said. "The leader is still alive and will get more braves who also hate the white man. He and the braves will take more scalps, but not today."

The mule and bay were hitched to the wagon and as it pulled away, the movement caused Chess to groan with pain. Eva, with the baby, sat close to him. She gave him sips of water from a canteen and checked to make sure his wounds didn't start bleeding.

Tom rode the dun, his hat sitting light on his head, covering the dried blood still in his hair and protecting the long scab from the arrow wound. Two Buffalo's paint was tied to the back of the wagon, along with the buckskin and Crow pony. The chief was driving the wagon with his loaded long rifle at his side.

They stopped at a slow-moving stream that night. The summer sun had warmed the water and Tom and Eva took advantage of it, taking a long bath in the clear water. She took her time washing the blood from Tom's hair, making sure not to remove part of the scab and start the scalp bleeding.

Naked, they sat together, holding each other as the water caressed their bodies. "I am sorry I put you in danger on this trip," he whispered.

Kissing his bearded cheek, she said, "You didn't put me in danger. I chose to come with you on the hunt. If it was our time, we would have died together. Instead, I was there to help load the rifles."

Scooping a hand full of water, Tom drizzled it down her back. "We should be getting back to camp. Our son will be hungry."

Climbing out of the water, they sat together on a blanket and let the evening breeze dry their glistening bodies. Running his hand over her soft skin, Tom told her, "Come morning, I'll come down to the stream and try and get some of the blood and fat out of the buckskins."

Moving his hand away, Eva began to dress. "Come morning, we'll burn the smelly buckskins."

* * *

It was late afternoon when the exhausted travelers arrived at the fort. The wooden stockade was located near the confluence of the Laramie and North Platte Rivers. The first stop was at the fort doctor. His formal training had been in dentistry, but working on the frontier had given him a good knowledge of treating wounds.

Chess slept most of the trip to the fort. Several times during the night he would cry out. During the day, Eva would ride next to him in the wagon and he only moaned when the wagon hit bigger bumps. She seemed to calm him by being near. It was possible he cried out at night more from fear than pain. Chess had been running a fever for the last two days and Eva had tried to help, bathing his face.

Tom pounded on the office door and a ruddy-faced man opened it. The doctor ran his fingers through his unruly gray hair. "What's all the racket?" he demanded.

"We have a wounded man here," Tom informed the old sawbones. "He was hit a couple times during a fight with some Crow."

"Damn unlucky, wasn't he?" the old doc said, chuckling at his own joke. "You say from the Crow? Aren't they friendly?"

"These ones weren't," Tom retorted. "They were anything but friendly."

They carried the semi-conscious Chess into the office and laid him on a narrow cot against the back wall. Quickly, the doctor began to cut the wounded man's clothing off to expose the injuries.

The office had a beat-up, roll-top desk with pigeon holes stuffed with papers and other odds and ends. A sturdy wooden chair sat in the middle of the room. Next to it was a small table with the gruesome tools used to extract teeth. The room smelled of lye. Dusty sacks of lime sat in one corner.

The old doc's name was Herbert Ward. He noticed Tom looking at the lime. "I had to cut off a freighter's leg this morning. He had a barrel crush it a week ago. It stunk up the room just awful. I dusted the place well with lime after hauling it out."

He then turned back to his work. Without looking up he said, "I will be here awhile. You can come back this evening, or tomorrow morning, and see how he is doing."

Leaving the doctor to his task, Tom stepped out of the small office. It was the first of August, and he needed to head for the Wind River soon. Eva was waiting with the cradleboard hanging on her back. Little Isaac was sleeping.

Returning to the wagon, he quickly told them what the doctor had said. Two Buffalo was readying the paint. He told Tom that his tribe would be having a gathering of elders. Having been their chief at one time, he wanted to go.

"Will you be gone long, Two Buffalo?" he asked his friend.

"I will be back in a week, maybe a little more." Swinging up onto the horse, he waved and rode away.

Eva walked beside her husband as he led the mule and buckskin across the compound and stopped the wagon in front of Louie's trading post. The building was filled with items needed by hunters and wagon trains. The smells of leather goods and new rope blended with the cooking spices and spilt rye. Metal traps and cookware hung on the log walls.

A grizzled, gray-haired man welcomed the travelers as they entered the low dwelling. "How was the hunt? You got a full wagon of hides, I suspect."

"We ran into Indian trouble on the way back," Tom said. "My partner was hit pretty badly."

"Two Buffalo was hurt?" Louie asked.

"No, it was Chess," he replied.

"Damn!" the concerned merchant said. "What Indians were they?"

"Crow. They were Crow. I think they were led by a mean-looking cuss with a scar running from his ear to his chin."

Shaking his head, Louie said, "That would be Red Wolf. He's a bad one. There are braves that follow him. They attack and kill emigrants that get separated from wagon trains or small groups of hunters. Most of the Crow are friendly with the white men. The army even uses them as scouts."

Eva stepped out from behind Tom, carrying the baby. Seeing the mother and child, worry changed to joy as Louie exclaimed, "You have had the baby! Come in! Come in and sit!"

The merchant led her to a chair near the potbelly stove. He poured hot water into a mug and added some tea. He set it next to Eva.

She was pale and tired from the birth and all that happened after, but she smiled and informed him, "It is a boy. His name is Isaac."

Louie slapped his hand on his knee. "Tom, you have a fine son and you have given him a good Christian name."

Tom smiled. "He is named after my brother. He was killed on the Ohio when we were traveling west."

Louie went to his shelves stacked with tin cups, can goods, and other neatly arranged items for sale. He selected several and put them into a bag. Coming back to Eva, he set the bag beside her. "Here are some things for you and the youngster. After we finish here, I want you to go see Lucy at the Buffalo Hide Saloon. She will get you a room at the boarding house, a gift from me."

Tom swallowed hard, hearing the generous offer from Louie. He knew his wife needed rest and good food to build back her strength, and with her nursing the child, it was even more important. Not trusting his voice, Tom smiled and nodded to the grizzled owner.

Walking back to the plank bar, the merchant set out a bottle of rye and glasses. "Have a drink and then we will talk business."

Tom accepted the rye, and tossed down his shot. The bite of the rye and warming in his stomach settled the emotions he had felt. Pouring a second, he waited for Louie to come back. "I haven't seen Two Buffalo. He is still with you, isn't he?" the burly man asked.

"Yes, he is," Tom said. "He went to visit some friends. He will be back before it is time to head out for the Wind River."

"We need to get a count of your hides and then . . ."

Tom held up his hand. "We lost the hides. They had to be left so we could lighten the wagon to run in front of the Crow."

Louie frowned. "Damn bad luck. A month's work shot. How are you set for the winter?"

Tom rubbed his whiskered chin. "There is enough from the first hunt to fund the winter trapping. I just have to hope it is a good season. I heard there are beaver in the Wind River area. With luck there will be some mink, fox, and wolf also."

"When you are ready to outfit yourself, I will give you my best prices," the merchant promised.

Tom went back to Eva and picked up the baby.

Turning back to Louie, he said, "We have a wagon outside that we can sell. If you know of any hunters that need one, let me know."

* * *

With the horses and mule put up at Louie's livery, they met with Lucy at the boarding house and got a room. Baths and clean clothing were the first things they needed. It was dark when they were finished. Lucy sent food over from the Buffalo Hide Saloon. The tired couple was grateful to eat at the boarding house.

Sitting in a gingham dress, Eva began to fuss with the baby. Tom, wearing dark wool pants and a green wool shirt, put on his flat-brimmed hat. He put on his holster with the Colt. Walking to the door, he paused and said, "I will be right back after checking on Chess."

The night air was cool as he walked toward the doctor's office. His footsteps were loud on the hard-packed path. Light from several dwellings outside the fort walls cut through the darkness.

A lamp was burning in the window of the office. Tom knocked lightly on the door. The tired old doc opened the door and motioned him in.

"Your friend should be alright. The fever was caused by the older wound on top of his shoulder. It wasn't properly taken care of and has some infection," the doctor said. "It will make recovery longer."

Looking toward the back of the room, Tom saw that there was a curtain in front of the cot. "Can I see Chess?"

"Make it quick. He needs rest now to let the

body fight the infection."

Pulling the curtain back, Tom looked at the pale, hollow-eyed face of his friend. Chess blinked, trying to focus on the mountain man.

"How are you feeling?" Tom asked, his face a mask of concern.

"Like hell," the wounded man said. "I don't even remember getting to the fort. When I awoke, I was looking up at the doc."

"You get well, Chess. I can get our supplies ready. We can take our time riding to the Wind River to save your strength," Tom offered.

His partner took a deep breath before answering. "I don't think I will be going with you this winter. The old man thinks it will be some months before I will be up and around."

Tom's face fell with the news. First it had been his brother Isaac, and now Chess who wouldn't be able to go. "Maybe another winter then, my friend."

The tall man left the doctor's office. The west wind was bringing in the smell of rain. As he walked toward the boarding house, he said a prayer for Chess' recovery. He had heard of less severe wounds going sour. He hoped that the dentist-doctor could pull his friend through.

Eva was in bed when he got back to the room. Baby Isaac lay next to her. She had left a lamp burning low on the table next to the bed. Seeing the two of them sleeping there made him think about his plan to spend the winter trapping.

He was fulfilling a dream that he and his brother had had back in Vermont. It was what had made them decide to travel to the frontier. They had not anticipated that one of them would die. Even more remote had been the thought that one would become a father so soon.

CHAPTER FOUR

Tom awoke to the sound of rain on the roof of the boarding house. Walking over to the window in his stocking feet and long johns, he looked out at the heavy, gray clouds.

Eva raised up on one elbow. Her black, shoulder-length hair hung loosely around her face. The baby began to squirm beside her. "Louie was very kind giving us this room for the night. We need to find a place of our own to stay."

Tom closed his eyes, trying to save the vision of how his wife and new mother looked this morning. Smiling, he said, "I will go up to the fort and see what's available. When I first came here, two men I was hunting with took a cabin for the winter. It might be empty."

While he dressed to leave, Eva changed the baby. Little Isaac cried in protest. Once he was cleaned up, she began to nurse him. Watching her work with the little one, Tom realized how much their lives had changed. No longer were they just responsible for themselves.

Putting his hat on, he said, "I will bring you some breakfast when I come back."

Walking out of the boarding house, he ducked his head against the blowing rain. The path he had walked up the night before was now slick and muddy. Hurrying over to the trading post, he stepped in out of the weather.

"Damn wet rain out there," he complained.

Louie laughed, "It's the only kind we have at Fort William."

Shaking the drops off his hat, Tom walked over to the potbelly stove. The warmth felt good. Soon his woolen shirt and pants were steaming. Louie brought him a tin cup to pour some coffee into.

Gripping the tin handle, Tom filled it and sipped the hot brew. "I would like to thank you for the room last night. We sure did need a good bath to get the stink of the buffalo hide off us."

"We have been friends now three, maybe four years. You narrowly escaped being killed out on the plain and needed a place to rest. I was pleased to be able to give you that," Louie said, trying to downplay the gesture.

Knowing that enough had been said, the tall man sat on the edge of a flour barrel and watched the merchant put items on the shelves.

"I'll be needing a place for the winter. I wondered if the one Gus and Hector stayed in was empty."

"That cabin burned last winter. A couple of easterners were staying there and knocked over an oil lamp while having a little disagreement. Damn shame, it was a well-built place." Pausing, Louie shook his head. "There are lots of folks with the American Fur Company up here. They're building a new fort up on the bluff near the river. It's going to have stone or adobe walls. I believe it will be called Fort John after a chap named John Sarpy."

"What will happen to this stockade?" Tom asked.

"We won't need it anymore. More than likely it will be torn down. Some of the wood will be used, most is in rough condition."

Tom would miss the welcome sight of the old stockade. Louie's trading post would still be here. The new fort would give trappers and hunters a place to sell their hides and resupply.

He knew that it would hurt his friend's business. The new fort would be a better defense against any attack. Fort William could easily be breached.

Tom selected a few items, including some canned peaches and dried apples. The trading post had some aged cheese. He added a chunk of this to his purchases. Louie placed two metal cups on the counter.

They were actually bigger than a normal tin cup. The bottom was a little larger than the top, to make it more stable. They had metal handles which were attached by wire rings at the upper lip, and rivets on the side of the mug.

"I just got these pannikins in. You can use them for drinking coffee, or cooking a small meal," Louie said, and he pushed them toward Tom.

Picking one up and giving it a close look, the tall man nodded. "These should work just fine on the mountain. Add a couple to my tally."

Carrying the items in a sack over his shoulder, he waved goodbye to Louie and headed back down the muddy path to the boarding house.

He found Eva enjoying a breakfast of biscuits with honey and hot tea. Looking up, she smiled. "Lucy brought us something to keep the chill off." Accepting a biscuit from her, Tom picked up the baby and sat next to her. Despite his worry, the squirming bundle in his arms was comforting.

Finishing the biscuit and licking the honey from his fingers, he stared at the floor and told her, "We may not be able to find a place for you and the baby in Fort William."

"Look at me, Tom," she said, her voice determined. "Don't worry, we can go with you this winter. I can help you with the drying of hides. The baby won't be any problem," she offered.

The Wind River Range had several tribes, some friendly with the trappers, some not. And not all white men traveling the mountains were honest. More than one trapper had been killed for his winter's catch.

"No, Eva," he said. "I need you and Isaac to stay near the fort, where it is safer."

"My family is three, maybe four day's ride north of here. The baby and I could go there," she suggested.

Tom knew that the Arapahoe and the Cheyenne were enemies of the Crow. But within the Arapahoe village she should be safe. That was a solution, if another could not be found.

They sat in the small boarding house room with the rain drumming on the roof as they discussed their options. Slowly, a plan formed.

It would be another month before he had to

head to the mountains. Tom suggested building a cabin. They would need a place at the end of the trapping season. With a family, they couldn't live under the stars.

Soon the decision was made. He would build them a home. Tom knew that there were many good stands of pine suitable for building a cabin near the North Platte River.

* * *

With the new plan, Tom changed his mind about selling the hide wagon. After checking on Chess and telling him of their plans, Tom got some lye from the doctor and gave the wagon a good scrubbing. With most of the smell from the hides gone, he traded with Louie for items necessary to build the cabin.

He sold Louie the hides not lost to the Crow. He kept two at the request of Eva. The merchant let him know about an area with available property for sale.

Using some of his share from the first buffalo hunt, Tom purchased 40 acres, which included a stand of lodge pole pine needed to build. It was a half-day's ride from the fort and only an hour from the nearest neighbor.

Before leaving, Tom made another visit to his partner at the doctor's. Chess, his face deathly pale, looked up at Tom. "Doc told me you become a land owner."

"Yep, now I have to build a cabin. If you like, I will bring your buckskin along. I plan to leave the Indian pony with Eva. I can just as easily build the animal's lean-to big enough for one more," Tom said.

Chess smiled weakly and said, "I would appreciate you doing that. If I leave the animal at the stable, Louie will own it soon."

Before departing, Tom talked to Doc Ward. The old man was sitting on a chair just outside the door, smoking his pipe.

"Chess is looking poorly," he said to the doctor.

"He had quite the fight the past couple days. I think the infection is gone. Now he has to get his strength back," the doc told him. "By the time you get back from the mountains he should be fit."

Hoping that the doctor was right, Tom went to the stable to collect the animals. Ralph the mule brayed when he saw his owner approach. Once they got to his property he would picket the horses and mule until he built a corral and found a pasture.

In the morning light the wagon stood ready to go. The mule and bay were hitched up. The buckskin, dun and pony were tied to the back of the wagon. Eva was holding the baby while Louie tried to get it to smile.

Tom finished some last minute checks. Louie wished them good health and went back into the trading post. After helping his wife into the wagon, he climbed alongside her and headed the wagon out of the fort.

The sky was blue, with puffy clouds making shadows on the plain. A warm, southerly breeze made the temperature comfortable. They squinted as the bright morning sun began its climb across the sky. It felt wonderful taking his family toward their new home. Tom hadn't known a home since leaving Vermont. They talked about what it would be like in their first place. Tom pointed out that the first hints of color were showing in some of the red maple.

It was early afternoon when they arrived at the property. It had a pond that they would build the cabin next to. The sky remained clear, promising a beautiful afternoon. The hill covered with pine rose to the west of them.

Experienced from a summer of moving and setting up new camps while buffalo hunting, they rapidly had their temporary camp set up. The horses and mule were picketed on the mature, brown grass. The troop tent was set up and a cook fire was crackling in a ring of stones.

After a short walk through the timber, Tom returned, satisfied with what he had found. Eva was busy at the fire, so he busied himself emptying the supplies from the wagon, which included metal hinges for the door and a small glass window to allow light into the main room. Reaching in, he pulled out a double-bit axe. Hefting it, he looked up the hill. Soon he would be up there, felling trees.

Eva stirred the pot over the fire. She called to Tom, "I have some soup ready for you. Come and eat, and then I will help you stow the supplies."

The pot contained chopped jerky and cattails roots she had dug near the pond. It was thickened with some corn meal. He noticed the Dutch oven on the fire. The smell of something sweet filled his nostrils.

The soup was bland, but hardy. He ate two helpings, dunking Louie's biscuits into the thick broth. He kept glancing at the Dutch oven, but Eva didn't open it or offer any of its contents with the meal.

"It is time to start on our cabin," he announced after they finished with the supplies. Eva smiled at the excitement that she saw in his eyes. She watched him pick up the axe and go get the mule. She didn't fully understand why they had to buy the land. Her people would put up a teepee, hunt an area, then move on.

The sound from Tom's axe rang out as he began cutting the pine. She heard several trees crash to the ground. The sound of him cutting them to length would follow. Eva was making him a special meal for their first night on their land.

Among the tall pine, Tom stood with his feet spread as he swung the axe at the tree. Large chunks of wood flew from the trunk as he buried the blade with each swing. After notching the tree on the side that he wanted it to fall on, he then moved to the other side and finished the chopping.

The first limbs of the pine were 30 feet off the ground, leaving perfect logs for building. Tom stepped back and looked at the trees that were ready to be skidded to their building site.

The cabin he planned to build would be modest in size. The two-room cabin would have a main room with a fireplace and a smaller room for a bed, or storage. Tom had driven stakes to mark the corners and, with the help of Eva and some string, they had squared them. The straight, limbless logs would require little hand hewing to make them fit tightly. It would save time in the construction.

Before he could lay the first log he would have to bring the wagon to an area he had noticed, an outcropping of rock. Tom would use the flat slabs of rock to lay a foundation for the logs. The first year the cabin would have a dirt floor. Once he returned from the winter's trapping, Tom would put in a proper floor.

Tom had chosen a site near the hill that would

protect the building from the cold, west wind. It was among a stand of trees, to make it less noticeable to riders passing by. The balsam trees around the cabin would be cleared for use in construction.

He arrived back at the camp dragging the first of many logs behind the mule. Eva had a ground cloth spread out with their meal, waiting for him. There were broiled fish, baked parsnips from Louie, and apple cobbler in the Dutch oven.

They sat with coffee after the satisfying meal, watching the sun set behind the hill. They both agreed that this would be a great place to raise Isaac.

"This year I will build a small cabin to get you through the winter. It will be comfortable, and will take less fuel to heat," Tom told her. "When I come back from trapping, I will add another section and we will have a fine home."

Eva leaned against Tom and rubbed his back. "It does not matter how big our cabin is. Just make sure you come back to us in the spring."

CHAPTER FIVE

Tom loaded several slabs of rock onto the wagon at the outcrop and drove the mule and buckskin back to the building site. He saw Eva next to the fire pit, working on the two buffalo hides. They were staked out on the ground, and she was busy scraping them before tanning them.

He laid a six-inch layer of stone for the foundation. On one end he began building the fireplace. He used stone and clay at the base. He would use clay-lined, split logs for the chimney.

Using the axe, he cut the first logs to length. Tom then used a broad axe to flatten two sides of the logs. He notched them and interlocked the logs on the stone foundation. He stood back and smiled at the result. He called to Eva, "We are on our way to moving into our new cabin."

It was the end of August and the cabin was shaping up nicely. The floor was packed dirt. The notched log walls fit tightly together. They had been chinked with moss and clay. Tom used a froe and froe club to hand-split shingles and planks.

Tom used some of these planks to make the door. He had already installed the single window, which offered adequate light in the main room. On the outside were shutters that could be closed over the window.

With the door finished, Tom led his wife into their new home. "Next year I will put in a plank floor."

Smiling, she looked at her broad-shouldered husband. "What we have here is all I want. My feet have touched earth all my life. It is a good thing."

He showed her the notched openings filled with blocks. These could be removed and used for defending the cabin if it was attacked.

The logs had been cut for the lean-to and corral. Once the cabin was done, he would build them. Eva, with the baby in the cradleboard on her back, had already spent hours cutting hay for the winter feed.

The cabin was small and snug. They would live and sleep in the main room. The smaller, second room would be used to store food and tools.

A stone hearth extended out from the fireplace. Tom had built a table and four stools, a bed, and some shelves for supplies. There were pegs on the wall for hanging coats and extra clothes. The furnishings had been rainy day work.

On a cold morning, Tom was notching the end of the logs for the lean-to when he saw movement on the horizon toward Fort William. A broad grin came to his face. It was Two Buffalo.

Swinging the axe into the log he was working on, he turned and ran to the cabin. "Eva, Eva! Two Buffalo is back."

She picked up Isaac, who was lying on the bed.

Hurrying outside, she stood next to her husband and waited for the rider to arrive.

Two Buffalo was carrying a young buck across the back of his saddle. "I heard you were building a cabin. I figured you would need meat to keep you strong."

He let the deer slide to the ground in front of the cabin and swung off the paint. Tom grasped his friend's hand and shook it vigorously. "Welcome to our home."

The white-haired chief looked at the log structure and nodded. "You are a fine builder. Your woman and son will be safe against the winter storms."

Tom had left one of the top logs extending out from a wall to hang game for skinning and butchering. Eva handed the baby to Tom and grabbed hold of the deer. She dragged it to the cabin.

Using a stick to spread the back legs, she tied a piece of rope to the stick and threw it over the extended log. Tom followed her and helped hoist the deer off the ground. She then sent him away.

"You have work to do on the lean-to. I will take care of this deer," Eva said.

Tom went back and led the paint to picket it with the other animals. He left Two Buffalo to strip the saddle and rub down the horse.

The lean-to was being built against the end of the cabin opposite the fireplace. The log structure would hold three horses. Eva would only have the pony and Chess' buckskin to winter.

By that evening the walls of the lean-to were up. In the morning he would work on the roof. A stack of split planks lay nearby, next to a pile of balsam poles. Tom used pegs or cut mortises to secure the rafters. He had purchased some cut nails to hold the planks.

That night Eva broiled venison steaks over a fire near the front of the cabin. Tom had encouraged her to use the fireplace to cook, but she preferred doing so over an open fire. A cast iron pot hung from a tripod and held beans to be eaten with the steaks.

After the meal, she presented him with a buffalo coat made from one of the hides kept from the hunt. "It will be cold in the Wind River area. This will keep you warm."

"I will think of you every time I put the coat on," he said, beaming from ear to ear.

During the next two weeks Tom completed the construction. The horses were in the split-rail corral. He now began his last chore, which was to cut enough wood for winter. Two Buffalo chose to hunt meat for the winter. One day, he came back to get the wagon to haul in a bear he had shot.

Eva would butcher the game the chief had brought in. Tom had finished making wood for the winter. Each night, after a busy day, they would clean up at the pond and retire shortly after sunset. One of the buffalo hides was spread on the floor. She planned to use the bear skin for a cover on the bed.

Two Buffalo slept in front of the fireplace while Tom and Eva used the bed. The baby slept in a cradle made by his father.

With their work done one evening, the family sat on a bench made of a split log and four legs. They were enjoying the sunset and making plans for their 40 acres. The two month-old Isaac was smiling at his mother's gentle teasing.

Two Buffalo came from feeding the horses.

"Have you talked to Eva?" he asked.

"Not yet," Tom said. "I had planned to wait for morning."

Looking at her husband, Eva asked, "What are you going to talk to me about?"

"It is time for Two Buffalo and me to head for the Wind River," he said.

There was a slight catch in her breath. "When? When do you plan to leave?"

"We will be going in two days," the white-haired chief replied. "A young brave and his wife from my tribe will be coming to stay with you for the winter."

Tom sat staring at his boots, unsure of what to say next. He had avoided the subject while building their cabin. She knew that they would be leaving soon.

Eva got up and put the baby into the cradleboard. She smoothed the creases out of her dress. Turning to her husband, she said, "We have much to do before you leave. Tonight we have the beauty of the evening to enjoy. We can start early tomorrow."

She then walked to the fire and refilled their coffee cups. Handing one to Tom, she sat close to him. Two Buffalo nodded and headed to the pond, leaving them to their private time.

CHAPTER SIX

The two men rode west, leading a pack horse and mule. The cold wind from the mountain range made them hunch down in their saddles. Leaves from the aspen and maple were showing the yellows and reds. They would soon be cascading down around the trunks.

Tom and Two Buffalo had left Fort William that morning after spending the night. They had looked in on Chess, who was on the mend. He was still too weak to make the trek into the mountains, but promised Tom that he would be ready for buffalo hunting in the spring.

Louie had promised to travel to the cabin, or send someone, at least once a month. They could bring them whatever supplies were needed. Tom could pay the bill come spring from his furs.

The young Cheyenne couple whom Two Buffalo brought to stay with Eva would be living in a cabin for the first time. Their mustangs were put into the corral. The window held a fascination for the

Cheyenne woman. The chief's proud nephew had assured Tom that he would keep them safe.

Tom had left a long rifle and the Mackinaw gun for hunting and defense. He had cast a number of .30 caliber pellets to be loaded into the smooth-bore Mackinaw. He had gotten a ramrod from Louie for loading the gun. The Mackinaw, with large shot, would provide a wide range of fire.

Confident that his family was in good hands, Tom, along with Two Buffalo, had left for the mountains. They'd followed the North Platte River. The trip had taken just over a week. The dun and paint had carried their riders with unerring steps, while the mule and bay, packed with traps, castor, and other supplies, had followed on lead ropes.

Tom pulled up the dun and sat, smelling the air. "We may see some rain, maybe snow before morning."

Two Buffalo agreed. "The wind brings us a warning of the coming storm. We have been climbing all day. The high peaks are already covered."

"The trapper that told us about the cabin on the Wind River warned us that it may need some work. It's been three years since he wintered in it," Tom said.

The horses continued ahead. The two men were outfitted for the extremes of the winter they would be facing. Tom was dressed in a buckskin shirt and pants. Eva had made him calf-high moccasins, with thick soles from the neck hide of the buffalo. The hair was on the inside, to give additional warmth. He also packed a pair of low-heeled, leather boots.

His brown, curly beard and moustache would protect his face from the winter bite. His hat was made from rabbit fur. The flaps on the side could be tied up off the ears during fairer weather. The buckskins, with a woolen shirt underneath, would be enough for most days. When the temperatures became frigid, he had the buffalo coat.

The Hawken was in the scabbard on his saddle. His Colt Paterson was in a holster under his coat. The handle of his skinning knife protruded from the top of his left moccasin. A possible bag hung at his side near his powder horn. It was filled with extra bullets, patches, Colt cylinders, flint and steel, and many other items needed for life in the mountains.

Two Buffalo chided Tom when he saw all of the things that he was bringing to the mountains. "A Cheyenne can leave with just a good knife, a deerskin cape to wear during the day and sleep in at night, and know how to survive in the wild."

"I see you wear a buckskin outfit and warm moccasins," Tom pointed out. "Plus that long rifle, and you have a bedroll for cold nights."

"I bring them to help take care of you," Two Buffalo said solemnly.

As they continued toward the Wind River, Tom knew that the success of the hunt would depend on the readiness and strength of both men. He also realized that the trapping know-how of the chief was critical.

They spent the night next to the North Platte River before breaking away along the Sweetwater River and over the foothills toward the Wind River. Tom built the fire and made coffee using beans ground before they'd left the fort.

Two Buffalo picketed the horses and mule. The animals had a thickening winter coat, giving them a rougher look. After finishing, he cut several boughs from a nearby grove of balsam and used some to make a windbreak by weaving them into the remaining branches. The rest he used to sleep on.

They made a meal out of fried side meat and hard bread. They hoped to hunt for some of their food during the trip. The wind that they had been bucking made it difficult to do.

With their meal eaten, the two men curled up in their blankets. Tom spread the buffalo hide coat over his blankets. The howl of the wind, along with the horses grazing and stomping, were comforting to the men as they drifted off to sleep.

Tom dreamt of bird feathers hitting his face. He sneezed as some caught on his nose. He woke suddenly and felt the large, heavy snowflakes hitting his face. The wind had settled down. He ducked his head under his blankets and drifted back to sleep.

Tom woke covered with a layer of fresh snow. He sat up, shaking the frozen precipitation from his coat and blankets. He noticed that Two Buffalo was already up. He had the fire going and water heating.

"We are still three days from the cabin where we will winter," Two Buffalo said. "This snow is a sign that our hunt will be good."

Tom didn't ask him why the snow was a good sign, but was willing to hope that it was true. Walking a short distance from the camp, he relieved himself. Returning to the fire, he felt invigorated by the freshness of the air. Little time was taken before breaking camp.

The chief shot a young buck that was in rut and was making a rub near some aspens. They stopped long enough to cut up the venison. They would enjoy steaks fried in the cast iron frying pan that night. Tom planned to mixed up some biscuits and baked them in the Dutch oven.

Two Buffalo put the deerskin on their packs. "The first one of the season."

"If we see any sign of beaver activity before we get to the cabin," Tom suggested, "we can stop and add some pelts to the pack."

The sun warmed their backs as they rode. The melting snow dripped from the trees around them. As they pushed through brush-covered ravines, chunks of wet snow rained down on the riders. By noon, the ground was mostly bare. Many of the leaves and some branches had come down with the weight of the snow.

The sound of elk bugling in the foothills had a chilling, lonely sound. Tom hoped that they could bag one of the large, antlered animals once they arrived at their winter camp. It would go a long way toward feeding them and providing bait for trapping wolf, martins, and other meat-eating animals. They would use these to supplement their beaver pelts.

The two men saw the pond in the basin ahead of them, several miles before they reached it. A stream flowing into the Sweetwater had been dammed by hard-working beaver. Several tree stumps stood near the water, chewed to a point by the sharp teeth of the large rodents.

Tom chose a location near the river to make their camp. It was about a half-mile from the beaver dam. The mountain man felt excitement course through him at the prospect of getting some pelts on their way to the winter cabin. While Two Buffalo scouted the pond for good locations to set their traps, Tom prepared the traps and cut aspen saplings for stakes to secure the chains.

Placing traps, stakes, castor, moccasins, and leather string onto the mule, the mountain man led it toward the pond. He met the chief coming back. "I found four places to set traps."

"We saw three lodges," Tom said. "With luck we should be able to catch six, maybe more, beaver."

"We must leave some to keep the pond active for future trapping," the chief warned him.

Tom stopped at the first location that Two Buffalo found. There was a short canal made by the beaver to exit the pond. The mountain man was wearing his low-cut boots. Removing them, he pulled on the moccasins. He entered the pond a short distance above the canal. Carrying a five-pound trap already set and a stake, he waded to the mouth of the exit.

Standing in the calf-deep cold water, he placed the trap on the bottom and then stretched out the chain, wading deeper into the pond. Tom placed the four-foot stake through the ring at the end of the chain and, using the hatchet in his belt, he drove it into the muddy bottom. After tying a leather string to the stake, he waded back to the exit of the canal and tied the other end to brush on the bank. He then pushed a bait stick into the bank and applied castor to the end of it.

Tom waded back above the canal and climbed out of the pond, water squishing in the moccasins and dripping off his buckskin britches. The plan was that when the beaver was drawn to the smell of castor on the bait stick it would step on the trap. The animal would then swim back into the pond, attempting to escape, and the weight of the trap would keep it at the bottom and it would drown.

The task was repeated at the other three sites

found by Two Buffalo. The two men then headed back for their camp site. There was the warning sound of a beaver tail slapping on the water as the men left the pond. A sharp-eyed animal had spotted them.

The mountain man removed his wet britches and pulled on a pair of woolen pants and replaced the moccasins with his low boots. The evening temperature was comfortable and the cold pond water had little affect on Tom. Later in the year, when his britches would freeze as soon as he climbed out of the water, he would have to huddle next to a fire to warm himself.

The chief started their cook fire while Tom put up a fly tarp for the two men to sleep under. After putting their packs under the edge, the mountain man led the stock to the river and watered them. By the time he finished Two Buffalo had a supper of side meat and coffee ready. Before adding grounds to the pot, he had filled his pannikin with the hot water and put tea into it.

Sitting near the fire, the two men talked of past hunts and trapping, reliving glory days. It was dark when they went to their blankets. Tom put his Hawken under the edge of his blanket and his Colt under his saddle. He fell asleep thinking of the traps set in the pond, wondering if they'd have any success overnight.

The basin was located in the Wind River Range and it was cold in the high country when Tom rolled out of his blankets. He could feel the warmth of banked coals under the layer of ash of last night's fire. Using tinder, he was able to coax the coals to light it and soon had flames lapping at the sticks he added.

With the fire going and a pot of water next to

the flames, Tom went to check on the horses. He had noticed that Two Buffalo was already gone from the camp when he'd awoke. He moved the animals to another area of grass and drove in their picket stakes.

He had tea steeping and the coffee ready by the time his friend returned. "We have three beaver," he informed Tom.

"I best make some hoops to dry them pelts after coffee and hard bread," the mountain man said, smiling.

The meal was quickly eaten and the hoops made from aspen saplings. Tom then donned his damp, buckskin britches and the cold moccasins. Arriving at the first canal, he found that that was one of the sites that had been successful. Wading into the pond, he pulled up the stake, taking care not to let the ring slip off the end. Gripping the chain, he pulled the 40-pound beaver to the bank.

Two Buffalo took the trap off the animal and reset the trap. Carefully handing it back to Tom, the mountain man waded back to place it back near the canal. Once the trap was staked and the castor applied, he climbed out of the pond to admire their first catch.

One of the other beavers went over 50 pounds, while the third was a younger one. With all the traps reset and their catch hanging from the sawbuck saddle on Ralph, the two men headed back toward the camp to skin the animals. The cold nights in the high country had made the beaver pelts prime. The castor was removed from the glands to add to their supply.

That night Tom roasted one of the beavers for their supper. The gamey, stringy meat was enjoyed by the men. Care had been taken to remove the fat, which would have given the meat a stronger taste. Leaning against the trees near their fire were the three pelts. Tom and the chief were in good spirits, having had success on their first attempt.

The two men spent a couple of more days at the pond and caught two more beavers. They decided that they'd come back this way in the spring and try their luck again. Having extra time in the afternoon, Tom cleaned and oiled his Colt and Hawken. Once finished he loaded them both, wanting them to be ready if needed.

The frost was thick on the grass when they awoke. Tom went to check on the horses and his mule. The frozen foliage crunched under his boots as he walked. The dun snorted and walked up to him. Rubbing the side of its neck, Tom paused and looked around the horizon.

The sun was just appearing in the east. The clear skies above promised a comfortable day. He shivered as the early morning cold cut through his wool shirt. He turned to go back to the fire.

He stopped when he noticed black smoke rising beyond the hill just south of them. Something large was burning. Hurrying back to the camp, he squatted next to the fire and held his arms over it for warmth.

"Damn, it's cold this morning," he complained.

Two Buffalo was frying more of the beaver. He looked around the camp. "The cold is good for the spirit. It makes us see and feel things we may miss otherwise."

Tom picked up his pannikin and filled it with steaming coffee. "Maybe that is why I was able to see the large cloud of smoke to the south," he kidded his friend.

Without looking up the chief said, "It might just be a cabin with a bad chimney. The morning fire ended up burning it down."

Enjoying the hot brew, Tom agreed. "You might be right."

"Of course, the sound of shots in the still morning air tells another story," Two Buffalo said, sliding the meat onto two tin plates. He handed one to the tall man.

"Shots?" Tom said. "I didn't hear gunshots this morning."

Cutting a slice of the crisp meat, the chief chewed it. Swallowing the food, he smiled and said, "It is good beaver." He looked toward the smoke. "It was just before you woke. Three shots with two different guns."

With the meal finished and their gear stowed, they brought the horses in. Smoothing the hair on the paint's back, the chief put the blanket and saddle onto the horse. He helped Tom lift the packs onto the bay and mule. The beaver pelts still drying on the hoops were hung on the sides of the packs.

Neither man spoke as they went through the routine. The smoke over the hill had disappeared. They would have to ride and check on the source. It could be a trapper or a family of immigrants who were attacked and had their place burned.

They might be wounded and in need of help. In the mountains, men couldn't just ride away if they saw another in trouble. There wasn't a marshal or doctor to come to their aid.

They crossed the river, leaving the pond behind, and headed toward the hill. The two men rode, leaving distance between themselves in case they rode into trouble. Stopping the horses on the crest of the hill, they looked into the valley below. A stream wound below them. The evergreens hid any evidence of the burnt structure.

The updraft of warming air in the valley brought the smell of smoke. The silence of the area below gave no clue of trouble ahead. The men rode part of the way down the hill before stopping.

They tied the pack animals in a grove of spruce trees. Checking their weapons one final time, they guided their horses toward the stream below. They rode with rifles across their saddles.

Two Buffalo stopped the paint and held up his hand. Swinging down, he glanced around before inspecting some hoof tracks. Tom could see the marks of several horses that had run along the bank of the stream.

Keeping his voice low, Tom asked, "How many horses?"

Standing and returning to his horse, Two Buffalo said, "There are five. Two were being ridden, and three led. They are only hours old."

The two men backtracked the running horses and soon caught a glimpse of the smoldering remains of a lean-to. Urging their horses forward, they saw the bodies of two people lying near the building.

It was a white man and a Flathead woman. Both had been scalped. Swinging down from their horses, Tom and Two Buffalo spread out and moved toward the bodies. An eerie stillness hung over the place.

Tom checked on the two people while the chief watched for unseen danger. Both victims had been shot in the back. Half-buried in some pine needles, the butt of a long rifle protruded. Checking it quickly, he noted that it had a spent cap.

Two Buffalo began to read the sign around the charred lean-to. Coming across a shovel, he picked it up and tossed it to the tall man. Without a word, Tom began digging graves.

With the couple buried, Tom stood at the graves and said some words over the departed. Two Buffalo stood a few paces away with his head bowed out of respect for the dead.

Walking back to their mounts, the chief shared his findings with Tom. "The woman was near the fire pit when the men rode in. She had been running towards the lean-to when she was shot. Her man fired his long rifle at the riders. He must have hit one. I found a piece of ear from the man that was hit." He made a motion across the top of the ear.

"The man was trying to help his woman and run when he was shot. After they killed them, the injured man sat near the fire while they bandaged his head." Two Buffalo pointed to the blood-spattered bench and the piece of ear.

"They took what furs there were and anything else of value from the lean-to before lighting it. The three horses being led came from the corral behind the building. They ate the meal she was making before they left."

Tom listened in silence. Looking around, he saw most of the sign that his friend had. He had noticed that one of the ridden horses was shod and the other was not. The people had been shot with large caliber weapons.

"Was it white men or Indians that did this?" he

asked.

"My guess would be white men," Two Buffalo said. "They were hunters or trappers."

They didn't find anything to identify the victims. The two men mounted their horses and rode back in the direction they had come from. The departing tracks of the killers were plain before them. The tall man knew that time was against them.

As if reading Tom's mind, Two Buffalo said, "We do not have the time to follow the men that did this."

"I know," Tom replied. "The most we can do is warn anyone we see about what happened. Warn them about the butchers."

Nodding, Two Buffalo replied, "Except for the men that did this."

Arriving at their pack animals, Tom suggested that they eat before moving on. Taking some biscuits and cheese from his saddlebags, he slung his canteen over his shoulder and joined the chief, who was sitting on a pine windfall.

Tom carried his skinning knife on his waist when wearing the low-heeled boots. Withdrawing it, he sliced a slab of cheese for himself and the chief. Placing his between the biscuit, he took a bite.

"I will follow the tracks a little farther and then meet you at tonight's camp," Two Buffalo told his friend.

Tom knew that they needed to know more about the killers, for their own safety. "If you catch up to them, don't take any chances."

Finishing the meal, Tom watched as Two Buffalo rode back into the valley to take up the trail. The tall man cut across the hillside to continue toward the Wind River. After two hours of riding, he caught sight of two buckskin-clad men sitting around a campfire.

Their horses were not in view. Tom's Hawken was in the saddle scabbard and would only provide him one shot. He decided to get closer and use the Colt if necessary. Pushing his coat back, he loosened the revolver.

"Hello, the camp!" he called out, pulling the dun to a stop.

The two trappers stood up and stepped apart. He noticed that one was holding a rifle pointed in his direction.

Cold realization swept over him. If these were the killers, then he had come in too close and they had the drop on him. The concern ebbed as he saw that both men had their ears intact.

"The name is Tom Franklin, I'm heading for the Wind River. Started smelling your coffee a ways back. Sure could use a cup."

The man with the rifle lowered it and said, "Set yourself down. I'm Cal Miller and my partner is Willis Green."

While drinking the coffee, Tom told the men about the killings at the lean-to. The man named Willis frowned. "That sounds like Wally and his Flathead woman. He come out about a month ago."

Cal emptied the grounds from their pot and kicked dirt over the fire. "You say one lost an ear?" he asked.

"Yep, I did. They have five horses. Only one is shod," Tom said.

Willis picked up his hat and crammed it onto his head. "It will be easy enough to recognize the sons-of-bitches. If we see 'em, we will shoot first and then hang 'em."

When Tom left the men, there were still a couple hours of daylight. He planned to ride another hour to the river before setting up camp. As he rode, he wondered how late it would be before the chief joined him.

CHAPTER SEVEN

Tom went to the Wind River and made camp. He put on a pot of water and beans. The horses and mule were watered and picketed on the grass-covered bank of the river.

As he stacked the packs next to the camp, the clank of the traps and cookware sounded loud in the cold evening air. He had finished eating and was drinking coffee when he heard a rider coming.

Moving into the shadows, he held the Hawken ready. His fire reflected off the approaching horse. He watched as the chief dismounted and loosened the saddle cinch. Tom stepped out from the trees.

"I was wondering how long you were going to hide in the woods before coming and take care of my horse," Two Buffalo kidded his partner.

"I would be happy to take care of the horse. I have beans and coffee near the fire for your supper," Tom said, taking the reins from the chief.

Taking his tin plate, Two Buffalo went to the cookpot and spooned out some beans. Sitting on the ground with the plate in his lap, he looked over to where Tom was rubbing down the horse.

"You make good beans. I might let you cook for us all winter," the chief teased.

"And if I didn't?" Tom challenged.

"I would then live on cold flour and pemmican," Two Buffalo replied.

"And you would live well on it," Tom said, finishing taking care of the paint. "But then our lean time supplies would be gone."

The tall man returned to the fire and poured another cup of coffee. "Tell me, what did you find?"

Two Buffalo rubbed sand on his tin plate and rinsed it in the river. Shaking off the excess water, he returned it to their packs. Tom patiently waited in the darkness for his friend.

Sitting together, sharing the warmth of the fire, Two Buffalo told him what he had found. "They rode hard for several miles. One of the horses they were leading was lost during the run. They stopped once to eat and change the bandage on the wound."

"The one that was shot is heavy and drags one foot. The other is thin and tall. He wears new boots and chews tobacco. Both men wear woolen pants. I followed them another hour before turning to meet with you."

Tom was always impressed at the amount of information his friend could gather from sign left behind. To Two Buffalo, a person resting in the dirt could leave a plain description.

The clear, star-studded sky gave warning of a cold night. Tom pulled out his buffalo coat and spread it over his blankets. In the next day or two he hoped to be at the cabin. It had a steep granite wall of rock towards the back. It was surrounded by spruce trees.

* * *

Two days later, they rode up to the cabin. The roof needed repair. Other than that, it was in good condition. There was no place to keep the horses out of the weather, so they would have to build a lean-to for them.

The granite wall rose up behind the cabin on the south side. The man who'd told them about the building had said that there was a cave in the rock large enough to store and dry their furs. Tom was happy to see that there was some grazing for the horses. They would have to cut and haul additional feed from surrounding meadows.

The door of the windowless cabin was in place, but needed to have the leather hinges replaced. An inspection of the fireplace confirmed that it was still lined with clay and functional. Tom could see daylight through the roof.

The cabin was furnished with a small plank table, two three-legged stools, and a log frame filled with old evergreen boughs that was used for a bed. Pegs were pounded into the log walls for hanging coats. One plank shelf offered a place to store a few goods.

Two of the roof rafters had split, allowing the cover slabs to sag and spread. There were spruce trees to make replacements. The leaking roof had done little damage to the inside of the small cabin.

"We need to make the place watertight first," Tom said.

Two Buffalo placed the pack he was carrying

in the corner of the cabin, away from the split rafters. "I will scout the streams and get some of our traps set while you do that."

Smiling, the tall man agreed. "After fixing the roof, maybe I will be able to find the cave and put our pelts in it."

The two men spent their first night sleeping under the stars in front of the cabin. The door was left open to air out the building. Tom had used the fireplace to make their evening meal. The heat of the fire would help remove the musty smell.

Two Buffalo rode away, leading the bay. Its pack contained traps, fresh-cut stakes to secure them, and castor. The steam of the horses' breath hung in the brisk morning air as they eagerly took to the trail.

Dressed in shirt sleeves, Tom selected three trees close to the cabin and soon had them limbed and peeled. Using one to prop up the sagging roof, he replaced the broken rafters. The gaps in the slabs closed as he forced them back up.

Satisfied that the roof would handle the coming winter's snow, he then felled several pine trees to build a shelter for the horses. The mule dragged them close to the cabin, where he cut them to length.

It was late afternoon when he finished chopping the logs. He got a fire going in the cabin and set water and beans to cook for his supper. There were still a couple hours of daylight, so he decided to search out the cave that he had been told about.

The base of the granite wall was littered with jagged pieces that had broken off during the subzero winters. A tangle of twisted and broken trees that had fallen from above lay rotting among the rocks.

Tom worked his way east along the wall,

climbing over obstacles as he searched for the cave. The going was slow as he hunted for an opening. Ahead, he saw a large slab of granite that had broken off the face. It was leaning against the face of the wall and the bottom had skidded out as it had hit the ground.

Walking past the large slab, he saw an opening on the far end. As he got closer, he noticed that the trees and rocks had been moved to provide an easier access to the gap. Tom found the opening was six feet wide at the base and narrowed as it went up to a point higher than he could reach.

As he moved inside, he passed charred wood from past fires. The opening went back over 20 feet, widening only slightly at the center. In the dim light at the back of the cave, he stumbled over a stack of rusting beaver traps. The cave had probably been used as a cache for trappers' gear.

Emerging back into the daylight, Tom squinted as he looked back toward the setting sun. He could not see the cabin from the cave, but did see a faint trail leading down toward the river.

Darkness would close quickly on the river valley once the sun went behind the mountain range. Tom went back by way of the trail. Several windfalls lay across the way. They could be an advantage, making the trail less obvious in case the cave was used for hiding.

The cabin was as he'd left it. Ralph the mule brayed as saw Tom. "You thirsty? I'll check on the beans and then water you."

After taking the animals to the stream running beside the cabin, he picketed them on fresh grass. He then carried the five beaver pelts to the cave. It was dark when he finished. Taking a moment, Tom looked up at the stars. Orion and several other constellations stood out in the late fall sky.

On the frontier, men had to learn to read the night sky to navigate on the rolling plains. Often when traveling, the wagon tongue was pointed at the North Star to help guide the next day. Moss on the trees, the wind, even which side snow sticks on an aspen can guide a man on a cloudy day.

Tom entered the cabin and added wood to the fireplace. The building was filled with the smell of the beans. As the wood caught fire, it lit the interior of the cabin. After placing a pot of water for coffee on the fire, he spooned the thick beans onto a tin plate.

Taking the food outside, he sat on a wooden bench. Blowing on the hot spoonful of beans, he tasted them. As he ate, he planned his work for the next day. The lean-to he would build would almost double the size of the building.

It had to hold four animals, in case of a severe storm. The lean-to would be built against the cabin. There would be sidewalls, but the outer wall would be left open to the east. The roof would be made of spruce poles. It would keep the snow off the animals and be a wind break.

With the beans eaten, he went back inside and added coffee to the boiling water. Soon, he sat at the table with the satisfying brew. He stared out the door, into the darkness, and wondered how Two Buffalo was doing.

CHAPTER EIGHT

When Two Buffalo rode away from the cabin, he glanced back and saw that Tom was already busy sharpening his axe for chopping trees. He didn't fully understand why his friend was driven to build cabins that could not be moved. Once the game and beavers were gone, it had to be left behind.

His tribe had lived in teepees that could be easily taken down and moved as needed. The fire was in the center, warming the inside evenly while the smoke went out the opening in the top.

The chief liked his tall friend, and had decided during the first winter that they'd met that he could accept this white man's ways. Two Buffalo's close family were gone, lost by time and battles. Tom and Eva were his new family.

Riding along the Wind River, he planned to set a trap line that would take a day by foot to travel, or a little less by horse. It would cover about five miles along streams flowing into the river. It would take him two to three days to lay it out.

Once done, he would set up another trap line for marten, wolves, bobcat, fisher, and others. It would have two trails out and back, each taking just over a half-day to walk. A shelter would have to be built at the far end to spend a night. A crude lean-to would be enough.

Guiding the paint along a stream, Two Buffalo found a beaver pond surrounded by aspen and cedar trees. It had several lodges. Leaving his animals tied to some tag alders, he put several traps, stakes, and the bottle of castor into a leather bag. Slinging it over his shoulder, he walked along the edge of the pond, looking for spots to put the traps.

The traps had been boiled with nuts and bark to remove the scent of man from them. The chief used a leather mitt to handle the metal traps to keep his smell off them. Once he found a site for the trap, he would spend as little time as possible in the area.

The soggy banks, cedar and other brush made the work slow. One at a time, he found spots that the beaver used to go to and from the pond. He set the traps and staked them. He sprinkled some of the castor to lure the beaver. Two Buffalo then blazed a tree near the traps to help locate the set easier.

By late afternoon he had three ponds set. Tired and chilled from fighting his way through the scrub brush around the cold ponds, he looked for a spot to spend the night. The sky was clear, so he wouldn't be dealing with rain or snow.

Finding a small meadow near the stream, he stripped the gear from the horses. The thick, rough coats of the animals would protect them from the coming frigid night. He used hobbles to prevent the horses from wandering too far. He then built a small fire to warm up and roast a rabbit he had shot earlier that day. His buckskin britches hung on a bush near the fire while he sat in his long johns, letting their legs dry while wearing them.

With the long johns dry enough, he pulled a pair of woolen pants from the pack and pulled them on. Stripping the skin off the rabbit, he rubbed on some salt and put it on a forked stick over the fire. Sitting back, Two Buffalo scraped the rabbit fur, removing the flesh and fat. The fur would make a fine hat or moccasin liner.

Taking a pannikin from his gear and filling it with water, he set it next to the fire for tea. While the meat roasted and the water heated, he sat back against a tree. It felt good to be back in the wild. The cedar-scented air and the sounds of the night were comforting.

After turning the meat to roast the other side, he took his skinning knife and cut a branch from the cedar. Creating a hoop, he stretched the rabbit fur over it. It would take a couple weeks to dry.

Two Buffalo added a few more sticks to the fire. From his saddle bag he removed a small tin. Taking a few tea leaves from it, he crumbled them into the pannikin to steep.

The rabbit was tender and moist as he pulled it apart and devoured the meat. While nursing the tea, he watched the moon come up. In the distance coyotes called to each other. The haunting screech of a mountain lion warned him that he had better bring the horses in closer to his camp.

After checking on the animals, Two Buffalo spread his ground tarp over some fallen cedar boughs. He put a blanket over this. His cape would be a top cover. With his fire taken care of and the horses settled down, he rolled up in his blankets.

Two Buffalo awoke at first light. In the crisp morning air, sound traveled a long way. He lay under his warm deerskin and blankets and listened to the forest wake up. A beaver was gnawing on an aspen, squirrels were rustling the leaves looking for nuts, chickadees sang in the brush.

Taking a handful of tinder that he had collected the night before, he placed it onto the gray ash of his banked fire. Blowing at the base of the tinder, some of the remaining coals started it smoking. Soon he had the fire going.

Sitting next to the fire with his deerskin cape wrapped around his shoulders, he fed wood into it. Looking up, he saw the horses next to the stream. Taking his pannikin cup, he went to fill it with water. There was a thin layer of ice next to the shore. Breaking it with the bottom of the pannikin, he dipped it in and took a drink. Refilling it, he set it next to the flames.

He hoped to find a couple of ponds on the next stream. He put the packs onto the bay before saddling the paint. It snorted and pushed the chief with its head.

"You like the mountain air, don't you?" he asked, rubbing the horse's shoulder.

As the chief rode away from the camp, there was little evidence that the meadow had been occupied. His friend Tom had often marveled at how Two Buffalo could travel through the land, leaving so little sign of his passing.

By midday, traps were set in two more ponds. Two Buffalo spent extra time constructing a deadfall trap, using an elevated log with a stick for a trigger. It was the method used by his ancestors, and still used if metal traps were not available. Once the prey ventured under the log to get the bait, the stick would be tripped, allowing the log to crush the animal.

They would move the traps to other ponds throughout the season as each became trapped out. It was time to set traps for the fishers, martens and others. The chief would work his way back past the ponds, setting the traps on leaning deadfalls. Meat would be used to bait them.

Two Buffalo had come across some porcupine near the last pond. He had shot two of them with his bow. The meat from the animals was on the pack horse. Working his way back along the beaver ponds, he set several traps on windfalls.

When he passed the ponds from the day before, he found four beaver in the traps. He stacked them on the pack horse. He would skin them at the end of the day. The chief wondered if Tom had found the cave. They would need someplace to store and dry the furs.

After spending another night on the trap line, Two Buffalo went back to the cabin. The beaver pelts would be stretched on frames, and the meat of one beaver to be saved for the men's meal.

Tom was binding spruce poles on the roof of the lean-to. They were not designed to keep rain out, but rather snow during the winter. He saw the chief coming and waved before scrambling down from the building.

"Are those beaver you got hanging on the packhorse?" Tom shouted as he ran to meet the chief.

"We have many ponds in the area," Two Buffalo said. "It should be a good year. We will miss having Chess to help."

Tom took the lead rope of the pack animal and led it toward the cabin. "You will be surprised how much I finished while you were gone."

The chief smiled as he followed the tall man. "If you are as good of a trapper as you are a builder, we will have much money come spring."

The lean-to was done, except for a little work remaining on the roof. Taking advantage of the standing trees, a good-sized corral had been erected. The horses and mule would have access to both. The men tied the paint and bay to one of the corral poles.

Tom had a pot of coffee on in the cabin. The two men poured their cups full and sat at the table. The chief noticed the repaired roof rafters and that the bed frame was filled with fresh evergreen boughs.

Two Buffalo sipped the strong brew. He preferred tea to coffee, but the hot drink was good. Tom brought out some hard bread and jerky.

"I have a beaver and some cattail roots for tonight. I will make a good soup for us," the chief promised.

"I found the cave," Tom said.

"Is it large enough to hold our furs?" Two Buffalo asked.

"It is large enough, and not too far away," the tall man answered.

While finishing their coffee, the chief told Tom about the trap line. Drawing in the dirt of the cabin floor with a stick from the kindling, he showed the layout.

"We still need to make the second trap line longer and build a shelter at the far end," Two Buffalo said.

"I will do that," Tom offered. "You did a lot of work already setting the traps in the ponds."

The chief knew that his friend had worked hard getting their base camp set up. It was obvious that he was anxious to start trapping.

After the meal, Tom took Two Buffalo to see the cave. He brought along a candle to allow them to explore the back. They found that the traps that the tall man had tripped on earlier were in good condition and could be useful on their trap line.

The cave would be a perfect place to store their furs. The trail from the cabin would have to be cleared. It would be visible to anyone passing the cabin. It would have to be so.

Returning to the cabin, Tom finished the lean-to while Two Buffalo took care of the horses and started the beaver soup. In the remaining hours of daylight they made hoops to stretch beaver pelts. Both men knew that the ponds would have to be checked every other day, at the very least.

From now until the ice was too thick for the beaver to break out, they would be busy. The second trap line would be checked twice a week. They decided that they would rotate on the longer overnight line.

After eating the beaver soup, the two men sat in front of the cabin drinking coffee. An owl called in the night. There was the yip of a fox hunting mice, and the familiar howling of the coyotes and wolves.

The men were up before daylight, had the horses saddled and the pack animals ready before they took time for breakfast. Tom made gruel with the cold flour. This and the coffee warmed them in the frigid morning air.

By the time the sun broke over the eastern

horizon, the men were riding the trap line. Tom and Two Buffalo rode together, checking on the beaver ponds. The trees had dropped most of their colorful leaves and the naked branches seemed to reach for the sky.

The first pond had one trap tripped. It contained a large male beaver. While Tom secured it on the pack horse, the chief reset the trap.

"We need to use some of the traps in the cave and make more sets on each pond," Two Buffalo said. "The pelts are in good condition. Soon the ice will close much of the shoreline for trapping."

"When I get back from the woods trap line, I'll boil some and get them ready for the beaver," Tom offered.

Grunting in agreement, the chief finished the set by adding some castor to the location. "Take care when you're laying out the woods line. You're carrying meat, and I heard the cry of the mountain cat on my last trip. I will not be there to save you if a cat catches you from behind."

Tom smiled, remembering the first winter trapping with his friend. A cougar had jumped him while he was skinning a beaver and the chief had come to his rescue, killing the animal with his bow.

"You have taught me well," the tall man said. "If a cat comes, I will bring you its skin."

As they rode to the next pond, the sharp sound of a beaver tail slapping the water warned the rest of the colony of the trappers' approach. The men continued to travel the pond trap line, completing the trip by midday. They had six beavers tied on the bay.

The two men sat around a small fire, drank coffee and chewed jerky. Two Buffalo skinned two of the beavers and went to put the bloody carcasses on the mule for Tom to bait traps.

"Cut the hind quarters and back straps from the smaller animal. I will eat that tonight," Tom requested.

"Make sure you trim the fat off the meat before you cook it. The fat can be strong," the chief warned him. Knowing this already, Tom smiled and nodded at his mentor.

With the meal finished and the bay packed, Two Buffalo headed back toward the cabin carrying his long rifle across the front of his saddle. Tom sat on the dun, holding the mule's lead rope.

He watched his elderly friend ride away. When they'd planned the trip to the Wind River area, Chess and Tom were going to do the trapping. The chief was going to stay near the cabin, take care of the furs and have meals ready for the tired trappers.

The tall man worried about putting this much burden on Two Buffalo. The chief had assured him that he could do his share. If the size of the trap lines became too difficult to cover, they could always shorten them.

Tom worked his way through the tree-covered valleys, following trails made by deer, wolves, and elk. He stopped several times and set traps on windfalls and other likely spots. He blazed the trees to mark the trap line.

He stopped near a stand of balsam that had several trees knocked down by wind or last winter's snow. Stripping the gear from the dun and mule, he picketed them on an area offering brown grass for grazing.

He walked around the tangle of trees, looking

for a good spot to build a simple lean-to for sleeping and storing emergency supplies. He chose a spot next to the stream above a clay slide. It was high enough to be safe from flooding, and secluded enough to stay hidden from prying eyes.

Tom cleared several windfalls from the area, dragging them to the side for use in building the shelter. Many of the downed trees were in the center of the stand of balsam. Once cleared, it would make an ideal area to keep the animals.

While the late afternoon air was cold, Tom was in shirt sleeves and sweating. He swung the axe in fluid motions as he limbed the evergreen trees. By the time the sun had set he had a stack of poles to build his shelter.

He put together a small fire and put his water-filled pannikin next to the flames to heat. He got the beaver meat and trimmed it. Then, slicing some salt pork into his frying pan, he cubed the beaver and added it to the pan.

The smell of the sizzling meat made his mouth water. He hadn't had anything but water since the jerky with Two Buffalo. Time had gotten away from him while cutting the balsam poles. It felt good to have the poles ready, but he would be making up his camp in the dark.

The sound of the mule braying startled Tom. The animals were still picketed below the clay slide. In his haste to work on the camp, he had forgotten about them. Grabbing his revolver, which was lying on a log next to the fire, he hurried toward the stream, stumbling over roots and stumps.

Stopping just short of the animals, he gasped for breath and struggled to hear any noise that might be causing his mule Ralph to bray. Eyes straining, he tried to identify the shadows in the area, searching for anything dangerous.

Finally, he gave up and went to the mule. Relief flooded over him when he determined that the braying was due to a tangled picket rope. The frustrated animal had given up trying to get loose and was demanding assistance.

"Damn you, Ralph," Tom scolded the mule. "You scared 10 years of life out of me. You're only supposed to holler if there is something bad sneaking up on us."

The tall man got the mule loose and then pulled the stake on the bay. He led the two animals up to the camp. He had a rope stretched between two trees. While tying them up for the night, there was a flash behind him. His meal in the frying pan was on fire!

Running to the fire, he grabbed the handle of the frying pan. Pulling it off the fire, he dropped the pan as the handle burnt his hand. "Son-of-a . . ." He shook the injured hand.

"For crying out loud!" Tom scolded himself. "You'd think this was your first night in the woods."

His meal was covered with ash from the fire. Brushing as much off as he could, Tom settled down to eat. The metal pannikin was ready for some tea leaves. Crushing them into the hot water, Tom set it onto the ground next to him.

Despite the ashes, the meal tasted quite good. The salt pork had seasoned it just enough. He had to favor the burnt palm on his right hand. It hadn't blistered, so by morning it should be okay. His calloused hands had protected him.

With the meal eaten, he set the frying pan on

the log. The hot tea was comforting in the crisp night air. Tired from the long day, Tom banked the fire and spread out his ground cloth and blankets. Using his saddle for his pillow, he laid down.

He placed his revolver under the saddle and his Hawken under the edge of his blanket. Sleep overtook Tom as his head hit the saddle. It seemed that he had just laid down when he awoke with a start.

Straining his ears and staring into the darkness, he couldn't figure out what had startled him. He realized that his animals were making no sound. Fear welled up in his chest. Had they been stolen? Indians, maybe?

Then, snarling brought him upright with the Colt in his hand. It was two animals fighting. There were animals fighting over something in his camp. The beaver meat!

Firing a shot in the air, he shouted, "Get the hell out of here!" He heard crashing in the brush from the intruders running from the camp. His guess was that it was bobcats, maybe even fishers.

Looking at the night sky, he saw that the sun would be up in another hour. He was too wound up now to go back to sleep. Pulling his boots on, Tom checked on the mule and bay. Then he put together a fire.

As the flames lapped around the sticks, he got a pot from the pack. Sticking the revolver into his waistband, he walked down to the stream and filled the pot with water. Kneeling at the water's edge, he scooped water with his hands to drink. Then, splashing some on his face, he stood for a moment, listening to the night sounds.

He could see his breath. The chill of the

morning began to cut through his long john top. Picking up the pot, he hurried back to his fire. Adding a little more wood, he set the pot next to the flames.

His shirt was still a little damp from sweating the night before. Picking up some sticks, he propped it up next to the fire. He huddled next to the crackling wood for warmth as he waited for his shirt to dry.

Daylight found the big man sitting with his blankets around his shoulders and drinking coffee. He looked around his camp. It was in shambles. Whatever had been after the meat had torn his pack open and spread many of the contents. He had left his axe lying near the stack of poles. The frying pan sat on the log, needing to be cleaned.

His shirt was finally dry. He slipped it on. Picking up the pan, Tom went and untied the animals and led them down to the stream for a drink. He watched the mule slurping water.

"What happened last night, Ralph? Weren't you supposed to let me know when the damn meat thieves came into camp?"

Ignoring the tall man, the mule moved away from the water and started tearing at some tender cedar boughs.

Tom let his horse and mule forage for food while cleaning the pan. Squatting on the sandy wedge near the stream, he used the abrasive grains to scour the pan. Rinsing it in the stream, he checked his work. It was evident that he would taste the ash for a while.

He staked the horses near the stream and went back to his camp. Picking up his bag of jerky, he tossed it back onto the pack. Tom knew that he had to finish the shelter and get back to setting traps.

By late morning Tom had the makeshift lean-to completed. A rectangular frame on the front was the entrance. Poles stacked against the frame made up the sloping roof. He tossed several of the balsam branches on top of the pole roof.

The low structure would be difficult to pick out in the stand of evergreen trees. Tom put a tin box toward the back of the lean-to containing flint, steel, powder, patches, bullets, and a knife for emergency use.

It was time to continue the woods trap line toward the cabin. Tom packed the mule and removed as much of the evidence that he had been there as possible. Setting out, he followed a winding valley that would bring him out just north of the cabin. Clouds were building above him as he traveled.

There was the smell of snow in the air. He was wearing a buckskin shirt over his wool shirt and long johns. The buffalo skin coat was back at the cabin. With the last trap set, he urged the dun to a trot, moving along the game trail.

Tag alders leaning over the trail tore at his face, arms and legs. The mule, with its lightened pack, followed effortlessly behind him. Large snowflakes began to fall. Tom was still an hour from the cabin.

He raised his head and took a deep breath of fresh air. There was a good chance that the snow from this storm could remain until spring. The valley that Tom was following ran behind the granite wall that rose near the cabin.

It came out on the Wind River, about a mile north of their winter camp. The wind was starting to pick up. The large flakes were now smaller, stinging pellets. By the time he arrived at the cabin, his beard and clothing were covered with snow.

He found the chief outside the cabin, tending to the fire. The Dutch oven was filled with browning biscuits. A deer hung in a tree next to the cabin. One of the hind quarters was roasting on a spit over the fire.

Looking up, Two Buffalo smiled. "This snow is ruining my plans of having a big meal waiting for you. It has slowed the roasting of the meat."

"Let me get these animals in the corral and I'll tell you about the new trap line," Tom said.

The dun and Ralph were happy to see the other two horses. They raced around the sides of the corral, kicking playfully in the snow.

Despite the weather's efforts to hamper the meal, the chief provided Tom with an excellent supper. The roasted venison haunch was crisp on the outside, with juicy meat on the inside. The sourdough biscuits went well with the meat.

The biggest surprise was sweetened rice for dessert. Two Buffalo had gotten a bag while at Fort William. Honey was used as a sweetener. The snow and wind continued, driving the men indoors. A coffee pot was on the crackling fireplace, the flames making shadows dance on the walls.

Tom sat against the wall, watching the fire. His cup of coffee sat on the floor next to him. The chief watched as his friend's eyes closed and his head tilted to one side.

"Proof of a good meal is a sleepy trapper," Two Buffalo said softly. He went out the door to check on the stock before going to sleep himself.

CHAPTER NINE

The snow stopped during the night. There was only a dusting on the ground. Two Buffalo left early to follow the pond trap line. Tom spent the day cutting the brown, mature hay in the mountain meadows. They would need the feed for the animals during periods of heavy snowfall.

Using one of the larger balsams and poles left over from the lean-to, Tom built a sledge with low sides to carry the hay. The mule pulled the sledge while Tom walked alongside. It allowed him to carry more hay down with each trip.

The tall man enjoyed working with the axe. Creating shelters and conveyances gave him a feeling of accomplishment. The dun was taken along to the meadow to allow it to graze. This would save the grass closer to their camp.

Returning with the second load of hay, Tom saw smoke rising through the trees near the cabin. He adjusted his Colt for easy access. More than likely Two Buffalo was back from the ponds, but he hadn't forgotten the dead trapper and his woman.

The chief sat next to the fire on a split-log bench. He was scraping one of the beaver pelts brought back from the ponds. There was a steaming pot of coffee on a flat rock next to the flames. Looking up, he saw his friend leading the mule.

"I see that you spent time building something to carry the hay. Why is it that the white man works to bring grass to the animals, rather than bring the animals to the grass?"

Grinning at his old friend, Tom replied, "Come a cold, miserable three-day blizzard, you will thank me for bringing this feed in. We will only have to leave the warm cabin just long enough to toss some hay to the animals. Then we scoot back into the warmth."

"Scoot? I do not think the Cheyenne scoot," Two Buffalo said, shaking his head. "I will let you go out in the storm and . . . scoot."

Tom stacked the load next to the corral, using a two-prong fork made out of an oak branch. He turned the dun and Ralph in with the other two horses. The chief walked over and looked at the sledge.

"This will work well if we get an elk. We won't have to lift the meat as high as the back of a horse. Maybe we will be lucky and shoot it near a road to the cabin."

"While you figure out the many ways to use the sledge, I will cut some steaks from the deer and get them cooking," Tom said, pulling his skinning knife.

Two Buffalo returned to the bench near the fire. He called over to the tall man, "We got four beaver today. I set eight more traps in the ponds. It should help. By the way, we also caught a bobcat and marten on the woods line that I came back on."

Returning to the fire with four steaks, Tom said, "I got a stack of stretching boards in the lean-to that we brought up from the fort. I'll get you a couple to fit the furs after I get this meat on."

Setting the frying pan onto the coals, Tom put a piece of salt pork into the pan and laid the steaks next to it. He climbed through the corral poles and selected two boards that would fit the furs.

He had a draw knife in the pack. Soon he planned to make a bench for clamping wood so that he could make more stretching boards.

Two Buffalo had poured two cups of coffee, and was using a stick to move the meat around in the pan, when Tom returned with the boards. The chief took them for the furs and handed the stick to the tall man.

While pulling the bobcat onto the board, Two Buffalo asked, "What are you using to cut the hay?"

After sipping the coffee, Tom replied, "I didn't bring a scythe, so I have been using the shingle froe. I got it good and sharp, and made the handle a little longer. It works just fine."

While the tall man finished the steaks, the chief went and got tin plates and some biscuits from the cabin. While they sat and ate, the sun went over the mountain and darkness closed in around them.

The stars were hidden by the cloud cover. Tom hoped that the snow would hold off so he could get more hay in. The sun had melted the snow off the meadow that he was cutting in. There were still patches of snow in the woods.

Before turning in, the two men led their stock to the stream. In the morning they would bring the furs to the cave. Tom would spend the next two days checking the traps on the woods line. The ponds had to be checked every other day, so Two Buffalo would spend his off day around the cabin.

Tom slept on the frame with evergreen boughs. Two Buffalo preferred sleeping near the fireplace. He laid his ground tarp on some cedar branches. They added some larger pieces of wood to the fire to help keep the cabin warm during the night. A bucket of water sat on the table for morning coffee. Tom snuffed out the candle and the men curled up under their blankets.

The tall man awoke. It was still dark in the cabin. The fire was out in the fireplace and the room was chilly. Crawling out of the bed of boughs, he sat on the edge and pulled his boots on.

He went out the door. Dawn was just breaking. Tom walked around the end of the cabin and relieved himself. He checked on the horses and mule. They stood together in the balsams.

Rubbing his arms to warm them, he went back into the cabin. Two Buffalo was getting the fire going. Tom stopped near the table and broke the ice on top of the bucket. He then filled the coffee pot and brought it to the fire.

"I will do some hunting today. If I get an elk, I will use the thing you built to haul it here," the chief said.

"You are welcome to use it, my friend. I am going to check the woods trap line, starting where I came out. Maybe I can meet you tomorrow at the last pond, and we can ride in together," Tom suggested.

"I have been hearing the big cat crying every night. Watch yourself and your animals," Two Buffalo warned.

It was well into the morning before Tom rode out, leading the mule. He was wearing his buckskins and the wool shirt. He had the buffalo skin coat tied to the back of his saddle with the bedroll. He wore his calf-high moccasins and his hat with the earflaps down.

He rode into a cutting north wind. The gray skies promised little sunshine for warmth. Small pools of water were frozen over and broke like shattered glass when the horse's hooves broke through them.

Tom checked several traps before finding a fisher. He opened the jaws of the trap and carefully removed the animal. While stiff, the fisher wasn't frozen. If it had been, he would have had to thaw it to prevent damaging the fur.

The next trap had a half-eaten raven. It had landed on the trap when going after the bait. Tracks showed that a marten had made a meal on the bird. While resetting the trap, Tom tossed the raven away in disgust. The animal that the bird had prevented them from catching would have brought more than a beaver pelt.

"Maybe the bugger will come back for a second helping," he muttered.

Tom arrived at the lean-to with three animals to skin. Along with the fisher, he'd caught a skunk and a bobcat. It was late in the season for a skunk. The smelly fur would bring a good price.

The dwelling was as he had left it. It still needed a way to close the front to keep blowing snow out. He dropped the pack off the mule, letting it and the dun wander loose to graze near the lean-to.

After getting the fire going, Tom went to the stream and filled his coffee pot. Climbing back up to the camp, he set it near the fire. While he waited for the water to heat, he selected some poles that he had cut on the previous trip.

Selecting two that were slightly longer than the opening was high, he lashed several longer poles to them. This would be the wall that he would lean against the opening when gone. If it was moved behind the fire when he used the lean-to, it would reflect the heat into the structure.

While sitting and eating his evening meal, the longing to be with his family weighed heavily on Tom. The reason he liked to keep busy was to push these thoughts out of his head. Sometimes he would dream about Eva and Isaac. He looked forward to those nights.

He noticed that the animals had wandered down near the stream. He walked over to fetch them back to the camp. The dun was still saddled, with the cinch loosened. Snow started to fall as he led them back to the camp.

He picketed them so that the balsam could be used to protect them from the snow. He leaned the wall against the opening. Pulling the bottom out, there was enough room to crawl in. Tom spread the ground cloth and blankets.

Then, removing his calf-high moccasins, he set them within easy reach. He curled up in the blankets with the buffalo coat as a cover. Before dozing, he checked the Colt under his saddle and the Hawken at his side.

It was still snowing when Tom awoke. He shivered after throwing off his covers. He pulled on the moccasins and his buckskin shirt. Pulling on his hat, he crawled out of the lean-to, dragging the buffalo skin coat behind him.

There were six inches of dense snow on the ground. He cleared it off the fire pit before making a small pile of twigs, moss and dry grass. Striking his flint with the steel, he sent a shower of sparks onto the tinder. It began to smolder and Tom blew on it as the grass slowly caught fire. His hands felt stiff in the frigid morning. Impatiently, he held them over the struggling fire, trying to warm them.

He made tea in his pannikin. He had two frozen biscuits that were warming on a rock near the fire. Tom went to check on the dun and mule before eating. He brushed the snow off their backs. Moving around was helping to warm him up.

After eating, he adjusted the wall in front of the lean-to. He had piled some wood and kindling inside for the next trip. Swinging into the saddle, he guided the horse and pack mule down to the stream. It felt good to be back on the dun, heading home.

He was thinking about meeting with Two Buffalo when he got to the first trap. It had a thrashing raccoon in it. Using a club from the pack, he struck the animal, putting an end to its struggles.

It was mid-morning when he came across the tracks of two horses. They were following the stream. Tom knew that it would lead to the pond that Two Buffalo was waiting at. The men were not in any hurry. The snow prevented reading any sign from them.

Huddled under the buffalo coat, he rode, hoping that it was trappers heading to someplace north of them on the Wind River. If he caught up to them, maybe they would have news from the fort. Word of mouth was the only way to keep up with things happening away from the mountains.

Temperatures were falling and the tall man's

breath was freezing on his beard. Tom caught the scent of smoke. He was near the location where Two Buffalo planned to wait for him. The riders had stopped and sat on their horses for a time. He guessed that they were deciding whether to ride around the camp, or to it.

He became alarmed when it appeared that the two riders had separated shortly after continuing. They were approaching the camp from two sides! Despite the frigid air, Tom opened his heavy coat to keep his Colt available. Across the saddle he carried the Hawken.

The fire came into view. Tom swung down from the dun and let the reins and lead rope fall to the snow. He stood, watching the camp. There was no sign of anyone, just the dying fire.

His initial fears were lowered a bit. The men he was following may have stopped and made their midday meal on this fire. Two Buffalo could be waiting on the other side of the pond.

Leaving his animals, he slowly walked toward the fire. The crunching of the snow under his feet was loud in his ears. Tom's heart pounded in his chest. He searched for any movement around the fire.

Standing a short distance from the camp, he read the visible sign. His worst fears were confirmed. There were tracks of additional horses. The snow was trampled, indicating that there had been some kind of confrontation.

Tom fought the emotion that he was feeling. He knew that he had to think. There was no blood on the snow. It was unlikely that the men had come up on the chief without him being aware of their approach.

The tracks of the riders departing the area were clear. They were leading two horses, Two Buffalo's horses. Using all of the discipline that he could muster, Tom moved around the camp, searching for clues of what had happened to his friend.

He found where the paint and bay had been tied. The tracks of one of the horses went away from the camp, crashing through the surrounding tag alders. Following the path of the horse, Tom saw something red on the snow. It was blood!

He went a few more steps, looking for more blood. He found none. He saw where one of the men had followed Two Buffalo's horse from the camp. He stood next to a windfall, his heart sinking.

It looked like Two Buffalo may have been wounded, but had managed to get on one of the horses. The men he had been following were chasing his injured friend.

With anger coursing through him, Tom stared after the tracks and vowed, "I will follow you bastards to the end of the earth and pay you in spades for hurting my friend!"

"Maybe I can help you deal the cards," a voice from under the windfall said.

The tall man almost slipped and fell as he whirled around to see the source of the voice. It was the chief! Tom pushed back the snow-covered brambles in front of the tree. Underneath, he saw his friend. There was blood on his buckskins.

"Damn, am I glad to see you! You scared me. I almost pissed myself when you spoke," Tom said, relief flooding over him. "How bad are you hit?" he asked as he reached to help Two Buffalo out of his hiding place.

"You did look pretty funny, jumping around like you were," Two Buffalo said, sniggering. "The bullet cut a gash across my leg, just below the hip. I think it will hurt more than it will harm me."

With the help of his tall friend, Two Buffalo limped toward the dying fire. Both men were smiling, knowing how easily it could have turned out much worse. Tom removed his buffalo skin coat and laid it onto the ground for the chief to sit on while he built up the fire.

"I was just finishing skinning the last beaver. For a while, I had heard the sound of two horses. I thought it would be you coming to have the rabbit I was roasting. Then I saw a rider coming through the trees. He held no weapon and waved as he got closer. My rifle lay next to the packs."

"Seeing only one horse and rider warned me something was not right. Then a stick broke from behind me. I moved to get to my rifle when I was hit. The bullet knocked my feet out from under me and I fell."

"I still had the knife in my hand. The bay was tied a few feet from me. I managed to cut the picket rope and get the animal running. The brush prevented the men from seeing me leap over the windfall and roll under it."

"The bay ran far enough before they caught it to keep them from figuring out where I got off. I could hear them talking. They found more blood beyond my hiding place. It must have been my blood dripping off the horse."

"I lay hidden and listened to the men as they laughed and went through the gear. They sat and ate the rabbit and talked of their good fortune coming across me near the pond. They planned to follow my tracks back to our camp and kill anyone there and add to their prize."

Tom put water on so that he could clean the wound. Then he began slicing side meat into the frying pan while he listened to the chief tell about the attack. Tom had no doubt that these were the same killers who had murdered the trapper and his woman. Anger surged through him as he thought about the cold-blooded killers.

Tom took his bedroll down from the dun and wrapped the blankets around the chief's shoulders. "I see they took your deerskin cape."

After cleaning the wound and tearing strips from the blanket to make a bandage, the two men sat drinking coffee and chewing the crisp meat.

"You can get to the cabin before the men," Two Buffalo said.

"And leave you here wounded?" Tom exclaimed. "I don't think so."

"I can ride. The wound isn't that bad," the chief insisted. "They will kill again. We were wrong not to go after them before."

Tom looked at this ashen-faced friend. "What if I go and the bleeding starts again, and you weaken and collapse on the snow? You would freeze before I could get back to you."

"When I meet the men on the other side, I will make their eternal rest anything but that," the chief assured him.

"Our things at the cabin aren't so important that the life of a friend could be traded," Tom said. "After I bring you back to the cabin, I will follow the men and send them to hell."

Two Buffalo looked at his young friend. "We cannot wait any longer and talk about what we might do. They will follow my winding trail to the cabin. You must cut straight across the hills. You will get there ahead of them and be waiting."

Tom knew that the chief was right. He also knew that if he didn't, Two Buffalo would try to make the ride. "I will leave you the dun and my Hawken. The Colt will take care of the cowards I am after. I will then come back for you across the hills."

A short time later, the tall man was riding bareback on the mule. He galloped Ralph across the tree-covered hills as he attempted to get ahead of the men. After a mile, he slowed the mule to a trot. It would do him no good to freeze the lungs of the animal and set himself afoot.

All was quiet at the cabin when Tom crossed the meadow to the east. He was thoroughly chilled in his buckskins and woolen underclothing. He walked the tired mule into the yard. His legs ached from clinging to the animal.

The only tracks he could see were those of the chief when he had left early that morning. Sliding off the animal, he tied it to the poles of the corral. He hurried into the cabin and got a fire going. Smoke coming from the chimney would give the killers confidence to ride in, expecting to catch him unaware.

Grabbing a blanket from the bed of boughs, he put it over his shoulders and went to the door. He looked and listened for any riders. Finding that all was quiet, he went out of the cabin, climbed through the corral poles and moved to the back of the cabin.

Sitting behind the building with the blanket to keep him warm, Tom waited. He realized that shortly he would be faced with killing two men, and possibly be killed in the process. Even a severely wounded man could still deliver a lethal shot.

The swirling wind blew the smoke from the chimney around him. He sat, shivering, knowing that the fireplace inside the cabin was making the room quite comfortable.

Through chattering teeth he said, "Having to leave my warm coat for my wounded friend will be another thing you bastards will have to answer for."

Tom was watching a chickadee that had landed on his moccasin when he heard the horses coming. He moved his cold, stiff fingers. He prayed that they would not fail him and that his aim would be straight.

In the wild frontier, justice was exacted by men willing to do so. There was not a sheriff or marshal to call upon to do the job. There were no judges to give out sentences.

While waiting for the riders to approach the cabin, he worried that these men might not have killed the trapper and his woman. They could just be men who killed Indians anywhere they found them. Whether it was right or wrong, it was not against the law.

Shaking his head, he knew that it mattered little. These men had tried to kill his friend. He heard their horses stop in front of the cabin. A voice called out.

"Hello, the cabin! You got any coffee in there for some cold travelers?"

Tom drew his Colt. It felt clumsy in his stiff fingers. He peeked around the corner of the building. In the yard were the two men, along with Two Buffalo's horses and gear. A stocky man sat on his pony, with the chief's long rifle lined up on the door. The other, thinner man held a revolver casually alongside his leg.

The man with the handgun called out again. "I am getting off my horse and gonna try your door. We're friendly and just looking for a place to spend the night. Now, don't be shooting me."

The long-legged man got off his roan and confidently walked to the cabin. His chubby friend with the rifle called after him, "Maybe the cabin is empty. Seeing the mule says someone is around, but maybe he's fetching some wood or hunting a meal."

Looking back, the man at the door said, "If so, we'll just wait in the cabin for him to come back. Maybe he will have something good for us to eat."

Tom saw that the mounted man holding the long rifle would have to turn his horse to bring the weapon to bear, or swing it across the animal to shoot at him. He would have to act before the other man entered the cabin.

Drawing a deep breath, he stepped forward, using the corner of the cabin as cover. "You sons-of-bitches looking for me? Drop your guns!"

He saw the shock on the two men's faces and they hesitated a second before reacting. The skinny man at the door turned, raising his revolver. Tom fired into the man. Trying to return fire, the man shot into the ground.

Tom stepped back to take cover behind the cabin when his foot turned on a rock under the snow. His legs went out from under him and he fell on his back, exposed to the two men. The fall saved his life. The mounted killer fired the long rifle and the bullet hit the cabin wall above Tom.

Lying on his back, Tom saw that the first man he'd shot was leaning on the cabin wall to stay upright, and was trying to aim the revolver. Tom shot him again. The man's knees buckled as he collapsed, landing on his back, in front of the door.

The fat man had dropped the empty rifle and wheeled his horse to make his escape. Tom swung his Colt at the mounted man and fired. His shot went wide and burned the rump of the pony. It bucked, unseating the portly rider. Tom scrambled back to his feet.

Despite his weight, the stocky man was quick to get up. His hat had come off when falling from the horse, revealing the missing ear. Digging under his coat, he pulled a Colt Paterson revolver.

He fired a snap shot in Tom's direction while scrambling toward some sparse brush. The man shouted, "You killed my brother! I will make you suffer for that."

Without answering, Tom leveled his Colt in the direction of the ranting man. He fired twice, hitting the fleeing man. Stumbling, the man fell to his hands and knees. Tom kept squeezing the trigger of the empty Colt. As if in slow motion, the chubby man limbs collapsed and he rolled onto his side.

The tall man stood staring at the two dead men in front of the cabin. He broke into a sweat as he realized how lucky he had been. What if his Colt had misfired? He had been driven by revenge. Tom walked to the cabin, kicking the dead man's arm out of the way as he entered.

In the cabin, he sat on a stool at the table. Tom realized that he had chosen to stop at nothing short of killing both men. He was okay with that.

Tom would have liked nothing more than to

shut out the carnage outside and stay in the warmth. He knew that it was impossible. First, he had to get the horses back into the corral. Then there was the matter of the bodies out front.

If Two Buffalo didn't show up at the cabin by the time he finished, he would backtrack and find him. Tom threw the corpses onto the sled and hitched the mule. Leading the animal, he walked away from the cabin, to a deep ravine.

He rolled the bodies into the crevasse and listened while they hit the rocks below. Tom hadn't even checked their pockets. Whatever they'd had was probably stolen. If someone happened by the rotting corpses come spring, they were welcome to whatever they could find.

While leading the mule down a rise near the cabin, Tom spotted the chief slowly approaching on the dun. His friend was hunched over the neck of the horse. It hurt him to see the proud Cheyenne in this shape.

Tom ran down the hill, pulling the mule while the sled bounced off rocks and stumps. Dropping the lead rope in front of the cabin, he went to meet Two Buffalo.

"Time to wake up, Two Buffalo," he kidded to cover his concern. "The horse has brought you home."

Coming alongside the rider, Tom reached up to steady the chief. The dun stopped beside the cabin. The tall man helped his friend down from the horse. Favoring the wounded leg, Two Buffalo leaned heavily on his friend. Motioning that he wanted to sit near the fireplace, Tom helped him sit on the skins that made up the bed.

"I sometimes think that I am too old for this trapping. Then I remember young Isaac back with your woman." Pausing before he spoke again, the chief said, "It is for him and his mother that we spend the winter trapping. It gave me the will to stay on the horse."

Tom added wood to the fire and put the coffee water on to heat. He put a second pot to heat so that he could clean his friend's wound. "I'll go and take care of the dun before putting a meal on and fixing you up."

Stepping outside the cabin, he left the door open to offer some light. Evidence of the spilt blood on the snow would be a reminder for the rest of the winter. The dun stood, with its head hanging, next to the corral.

"I see you're looking to get in there with your friends," he said, patting it on the shoulder. Stripping the saddle and bridle from the animal, he lowered the corral poles and let the horse in. He then unhooked the mule and led it in.

While taking the halter off, he said, "You did a good job getting me back here ahead of those men." Snorting as though to answer Tom, the mule pushed by him.

Tom tossed some hay into the lean-to for the horses and mule to eat. Ralph rushed toward the feed, pushing the horses out of the way. Prodding the mule with the wooden fork, he said, "Take your turn, you ornery cuss." Then, smiling, he said, "Ah hell, go for it, you earned it."

CHAPTER TEN

Tom spent most of his time working the beaver pond while Two Buffalo healed, traveling a shortened woods trap line when returning from the last pond. The chief sat near the front door of the cabin, scraping and stretching the furs for drying. The cave behind the cabin was building up a nice stock for sale in the spring.

The additional horses from the two killers put an extra burden on the hay that Tom had put up for the winter. On the clear days, the chief drove the horses up to the high meadows to spend the day grazing, while the tall man checked the traps.

Tom rotated the horses that he rode on the trap line but always used Ralph the mule as a pack animal. He trusted it to warn him of danger. Often, he wouldn't even need a rope, and the mule would follow whatever horse Tom was riding.

In the wooded areas the horse would struggle, breaking through the crust of the belly-deep snow. Relief would come in the open areas, where the trail remained open due to windblown snow.

A combination of shorter daylight and setting the traps in the frigid water took more time, and Tom would often get back after dark. Two Buffalo would have a fire burning in front of the cabin to guide him through the darkness.

After a two-day snowstorm, the men woke to a clear and bright morning. Tom prepared to ride the paint to check the traps.

"I will take the horses up to the south meadow today," Two Buffalo said, squinting from the sunlight reflecting off the snow.

"I heard the cat again during the night. Check for tracks in the new snow. Maybe we can set some traps for it," Tom suggested.

Two Buffalo saddled the roan. "We are low on meat. Bring back a couple of beaver. I'll have a pot of beans on the fire. We can roast one of them and make a fine meal."

The mule stood next to the paint, ready to follow. Tom noticed that the wood pile needed to be replenished. If the weather permitted, he would spend the next day cutting and splitting.

The long-legged paint broke trail easily as he headed for the first pond. Tom sat with the Hawken across the saddle. The heavy buffalo coat kept the morning chill out.

As close as they could estimate, it was after Christmas. The winter still had a long way to go before the warmth of spring would come. The furs that they were getting were in prime condition with their winter coat. Two Buffalo could start traveling the beaver trap line again and leave Tom free to return to the inland trap line.

Any new snow made checking and resetting the traps difficult on the open, spring fed ponds. Even a dusting of snow covered the movements of the beaver as they came out to feed on the nearby saplings.

The trip netted three large beaver pelts. The sun was just above the western mountains when he finished with the last pond.

"Two Buffalo will have to wait until tomorrow for the roasted beaver," he said to Ralph as he secured the pack. "It will be near midnight when we get back."

Tom swung onto the paint and started back to the cabin. He could take the same route that he'd beaten the killers with; but in the dark, after the snow, getting lost was almost a certainty. He had to follow their trail back to the cabin.

The sure-footed horse moved along the back trail with little urging. The tall man glanced at the sun sliding behind the mountains. He raised his face to the sky and sniffed the air.

"Damn the luck," he muttered. "It smells like another storm is coming in."

As he rode toward the warmth of the cabin, the stars appeared in the eastern night sky. Storm clouds were building in the west. Tom knew that the moon would come up in about an hour. Being near full, it would provide enough light to see the trail. That is, until it was covered by the snow clouds coming in.

* * *

While his friend worked his way back from the beaver ponds, Two Buffalo sat next to the stiffening remains of the elk he had shot. Three hours earlier, he had just started to round up the grazing horses when

110

he had spotted a young bull elk.

The meat from this one animal would feed him and Tom for a month. The animal had had the waning sun behind it. Two Buffalo had knelt, bringing the long rifle to bear on the shoulder of the elk.

The shot had impacted further behind the shoulder than planned. Leaping forward, the elk had run across the meadow, heading for the safety of the pines.

Having taken a moment to reload the long rifle, the chief had then mounted the roan and galloped after the wounded animal. The blood trail along the tracks of the running animal had assured Two Buffalo that it was a fatal shot. The question had been how long it would take for the elk to bleed out.

Once in the pines, he had slowed the horse to a walk. The bleeding had decreased, and the deepening shadows of the forest had made following the wounded animal's tracks difficult among the crisscrossing trails of other wandering animals.

Dismounting from the roan, he had walked to help identify the elk's tracks. There had been the sound of a running animal in the dusk ahead. He had found where the elk had laid, weakening from the wound. Hearing the chief coming, it had once again run.

All of a sudden, there had been movement and the sound of a snarling cougar. He'd seen the staggering elk collapse under the weight of the mountain cat that jumped onto its back. Without hesitation, Two Buffalo had dropped the reins, brought the rifle to his shoulder and squeezed the trigger.

The bullet had hit the large cat and sent it

running and screeching from the elk. After a short distance it had fallen, writhing in its death struggle.

Standing in the dark, Two Buffalo saw the silhouettes of the two downed animals lying on the snow. Turning, he'd seen that the roan had run out of sight when he'd fired at the cat. After loading his weapon, Two Buffalo had walked up to the elk and prodded it with the end of the rifle. It was dead.

Now he sat in the dark, next to enough meat to last a month. The cougar would provide meat and a high-priced skin.

If he went to find the horse, he would risk the downed animals being discovered by wolves. In short order, a pack of hungry wolves could tear the elk apart, destroying much of the meat. They would also go after the cat, ruining the skin too.

The moon was just breaking the eastern horizon. The howls of the wolves cut through the night air. He knew that they were tracking the wounded elk. The chief went over to the cougar and dragged the heavy cat next to the elk.

He broke several pine branches and found some moss and other tinder. Two Buffalo knelt to strike his flint. The moss began to smoke and he bent over to blow on it.

The heavy body of a wolf hit him on the back, missing its target, which was the back of his neck. The motion to blow on the tinder had saved him from having the gray wolf sink its teeth into his spine.

The chief rolled forward over his pile of wood, clear of the wolf. The wolf jumped on the elk and lay snarling, protecting its prey. The long rifle lay within reach of Two Buffalo. He picked it up and swung the barrel at the gray hulk.

Yelping, the wolf abandoned the kill, turned and growled as it circled the chief. Two Buffalo knew that it would only be moments and more wolves would arrive. Driven by the smell of blood and their hunger, they would lose all fear of man.

The flicker of the tinder catching fire caught his eye. He moved near the stack of pine branches and pushed them over the tinder. Holding the rifle level, he watched the gray beast prepare to leap.

Two Buffalo fired into the chest of the wolf, sending it stumbling back, crying. The flash of the powder burning and the report of the gun stopped the rest of the pack, which was now in sight.

The pine branch quickly caught fire, lighting up the area. The glow of the wolves' eyes were all around him. There were at least five trying to get at the downed animals.

Years in the wild country had taught him to remain calm. Two Buffalo reloaded the long rifle. It would be only a few minutes before the dry branches burned down. Then the wolves would overcome their fear and attack.

One of the wolves sat a short distance away from the rest, watching and waiting. The chief raised the rifle and shot it. The animal did a somersault and fell dead on the snow. Once again, the sound of the rifle sent the rest of the wolves running a short distance away.

After reloading the rifle, Two Buffalo looked around for more wood. A dead, smaller pine stood a few paces away. Hurrying to the tree, he pushed it, trying to break it off in the direction of the fire. There was a snap as the brittle trunk broke.

He ripped the top parts of the tree off and built

up his fire. He looked away from the fire and waited for his eyes to adjust to the darkness. The sounds of the wolves fighting over the one he had shot reached his ears.

There was enough wood to keep the fire going for a couple of hours. The pine burnt quickly, with its sap snapping, sending showers of sparks into the air. The wolves moved away from the ravaged carcass and circled Two Buffalo.

They were keeping just outside of the ring of firelight, within the stand of pine trees. The chief went and pulled the dead cougar closer to the fire. There was a chance that an aggressive wolf might attempt to run in and grab at a dead animal, attempting to gain a mouthful of meat.

Two Buffalo shook his powder horn and checked for bullets in his possible bag. He had another eight or ten loads for the long rifle. It would help to keep the wolves away for a while, but once his fire burnt down they would charge and he would only get one shot off.

Sitting in the snow next to the fire, the chief looked for a tree he could use to climb to safety. The pine around him were mostly over a foot in diameter, and the lowest branches were over 20 feet from the ground.

A few smaller pines fought to survive under the umbrella of the larger ones, but they would hardly carry his weight. Two Buffalo broke a three-foot chunk off the dead tree he was burning.

Once he had used up the supply of wood, he would get the chunk burning and use it to get away from the wolves. The dead cat and elk should keep them busy while he looked for a safe place to hole up until daylight.

Out of the darkness came the howls and snarling of the wolves around him. Farther off, he heard others answering. He knew that more hungry wolves would join the pack.

For an hour he kept pulling the downed pine over the fire as it burnt off. Alone in the darkness, he knew that he had made a mistake staying with the elk and cougar. When he'd shot the cougar, he hadn't expect the roan to run.

Anyone who had spent any amount of time in the mountains knew that one of the dangers when hunting was getting your game out before wolves or coyotes got wind of the kill. Two Buffalo knew this, but the thought of surprising Tom with fresh meat had made him forget for the moment.

The pine that he was burning was growing short. It was still several hours before daylight. It was time to get ready for the escape attempt. Pulling the last piece of tree onto the fire, he set the short chunk next to the coals to light.

Tending to the fire blinded the chief in the darkness. Sitting with his long rifle across his lap, he raised his arms and face to the cloud-covered sky. He began to sing his death song.

The chorus of the wolves competed in the night air. Two Buffalo thought about all those whom he had sent to the other side and would be waiting for him. He sang for strength to defend his place there against his enemies.

The loud crack of a rifle broke through the noise of the wolves and the chief's song. He heard the sound of shouting and running horses. It was Tom!

The tall man rode in, leading the roan with one

hand and firing his Colt at the wolves with the other. Stopping the paint near the fire, he swung his leg over the horse's head and slid to the ground.

"This is a hell of a spot you got yourself into!" he shouted to his friend while pulling the Hawken from the saddle.

"I am glad you are here. I was just about to start broiling some steaks from the elk for you," Two Buffalo said. "Unless you would rather have beaver."

Tom looked at the young bull elk and the cougar. "This is too damn much meat to leave for the wolves." Pulling his skinning knife, he cut the hind quarters and back straps off the elk.

Two Buffalo held the horses while the tall man loaded the meat onto the roan. He then hung the cat over the elk meat, securing them to the saddle with a horse hair rope. He could hear the scattered wolves returning. The smell of blood was stronger now and soon their fears of the fire would be overcome by the desire to get at the meat.

The elk meat and cougar weighed over 200 pounds and was all the roan could carry. Putting a fresh cylinder into the Colt and sliding his Hawken into the scabbard, he swung up onto the paint. Reaching down, he offered a hand and pulled his friend up behind him.

With the chief holding the reins of the roan, Tom urged the paint back toward the cabin, leaving the fire and wolves behind. One of the wolves leaped out and tried to grab at the elk meat on the roan. Two Buffalo emptied the long rifle at the animal, hitting it in the lower side, sending it rolling and kicking in the snow.

In the feeble moonlight that was able to

penetrate the cloud cover, the two men rode across the meadow and onto the trail leading them back to the cabin. It was only two miles from the meadow to the cabin.

The short trip seemed to take forever in the darkness. At any moment the men expected to have wolves come up from behind and try to hamstring the roan. They reached the safety of the cabin and stopped in front of the door.

The men got off the horse and quickly dragged the elk and cougar into the cabin. The chief went to the fireplace to light it while Tom went back outside to pull the gear off the horses and put them into the corral.

He tossed some hay into the lean-to for the animals to keep them close to the cabin. There was always the chance that the wolves would follow the scent of the kills. Tom could depend on the mule to warn him.

He went back into the cabin. Two Buffalo had the fire going and water heating for coffee. He had cut some steaks out of the back straps and had just set them into the black cast iron frying pan.

"It is good that you came when you did," the chief admitted. "I was sure that soon I would be a meal for the wolves."

Tom moved the elk hindquarters and the cat away from the center of the room. He sat on a stool at the table and looked at his old friend.

"I came back from the ponds expecting to find you asleep and a pot of beans keeping warm next to the coals. When I found the fire out and our extra horses eating from the haystack, I knew something was wrong."

"First I checked the cabin, expected to find you injured. I thought you had not been able to put the stock in the corral. When I found the cabin empty, I then feared I had lost my best friend. It was obvious that the horses had come back on their own. I put them and the mule in the corral and headed for the meadow to find you."

"I could hear wolves howling all around me as I rode. I prayed real hard that I would find you before the hungry animals did. The meadow was empty except for the roan walking, dragging its reins. I could hear the pack that had you cornered setting up a ruckus."

"It was too dark to see any tracks, so I just followed the sounds of the wolves. Shortly after entering the trees, I caught sight of the burst of sparks when you added wood to the fire. I can't tell you how good that made me feel, knowing you weren't dead."

"Guiding the horse with my knees, I pulled the Colt and headed for your fire. I heard you singing your death song and it plain made me mad at the wolves. I spurred the horse along and started shooting at every moving shadow I saw."

Two Buffalo sat in silence, listening to his tall friend. He regretted that he had caused Tom concern. "It was late and I should not have shot at the elk. I cannot blame the wolves for the trouble I was in."

Both men knew enough had been said about the events of the day. They had meat to take care of, a cat to skin, and beaver pelts to stretch, and both were tired from missing a night's sleep. While Tom finished making their meal, Two Buffalo skinned the cougar.

"Tomorrow I will make you a tasty soup with the cougar meat," the chief promised.

CHAPTER ELEVEN

The men set traps around the cabin for wolves and caught seven that were drawn to their livestock and meat larder. They hung the meat in a tall pine next to the cabin, to keep it away from wildlife. When the wind brought the smell of wolves Ralph would bray loudly, alerting the men.

Two Buffalo went back to the ponds, setting traps in a few places that stayed open due to springs. Several of their traps were under the ice and they would have to wait for the spring thaw to retrieve them. Tom spent his time along the forest line. The month of February started with temperatures well below zero. The men nearly froze trying to keep warm in the cabin.

At least one day a week had to be dedicated to cutting wood for their fires. Two Buffalo preferred to cook over the fire pit in front of the cabin. Often, both the fireplace and the fire pit were burning.

They had a visitor for a few days. A trapper named Barnet had his cabin burn down. He had lost most of his furs and much of his gear. He was riding an underfed Indian pony and leading an equally rough-looking packhorse.

His saddle was a pad stuffed with grass, commonly used by the Blackfoot. Tom gave him the pony and one of the saddles gotten from the killers. They sent the man on his way with enough food to get to Fort William and with a letter for Eva.

Two days after Barnet left, Tom readied the mule before heading out to run the trap line. Two Buffalo had already left to search for any open water near the beaver ponds and expected to find that the cold spell had frozen everything over. The frigid temperatures had finally rose a bit and there was the smell of snow in the air.

Tom decided to walk and lead Ralph instead of riding the dun. The cold had kept them sitting around the cabin too much and he needed a good, long walk to limber up his legs. If he got tired, he could always climb onto the mule.

He put the warm buffalo skin coat on and carried his canteen under the coat on one side to prevent it from freezing. On the other side Tom carried his possible bag, which contained various items, including his food.

Pulling the cabin door shut, he took the lead rope and headed for the first trap set. Tom didn't expect to find too many catches. Not much moved around during frigid weather. The bait would be frozen solid and would give off little smell to draw animals in.

The frozen trail was rough from the winter travel and made walking on the snow difficult. The cold had created a thick crust on the snow, so Tom walked alongside the trail. While the crust supported his weight, the mule would break through. He tossed the lead rope over the packs and let it stay on the rough-packed trail.

It was not until the fifth trap that there was success. A nicely sized bobcat hung from the sprung trap. Taking his time, Tom opened the trap and removed the frozen animal.

After his midday meal, he had to take the coat off and tie it onto the mule. He didn't want to start sweating. Soon after a man started to perspire in the frosty temperatures, he would get the chills. Death could soon follow.

He felt good about the day's walk. It yielded the bobcat and two martens. Tom arrived at the crude lean-to and pulled the front wall back. He reached in to take a handful of kindling.

Movement from inside made him jump back. Several large-eared mice ran from the pile of sticks. "Damn little critters taking up housekeeping in my lean-to!" he exclaimed.

Grabbing one of the bigger sticks, he crawled into the shelter and did his best to club at a few of them. The frightened rodents successfully eluded Tom and were soon safely out of reach in the depths of the lean-to.

Emerging from his futile attempt at the mice, Tom looked over at Ralph waiting to be unloaded. "The damn little buggers sure are fast. Now I will be sleeping with them," he said to the indifferent mule.

Tom rustled the kindling pile before picking a bunch for the fire, just in case one or two mice had lagged behind. Once he had the fire going, he pulled the packs off the mule. He left it to Ralph to search for something to graze on. Tom slipped and slid down to the stream to fill his cook pot with water.

After the long cold spell, the water was frozen nearly to the bottom of the stream. Giving up on finding an open spot, Tom filled the pot with snow and brought it back to the fire.

While waiting for the melted snow to heat up, he hunted up enough wood for the evening and morning fires. With the sun going down, the temperature was dropping rapidly. Tom sat next to the crackling fire to keep warm.

He had his catch near the fire to thaw them enough so that they could be skinned. A light snow began to fall. Tom liked to sit with his back to the fire and watch the light reflect off the flakes.

Once the water was hot, he poured the steaming liquid into his pannikin and added some tea leaves. He took some cold rabbit from his possible bag and put it on a stick, heating it over the fire.

The mule, wanting some company, had wandered back near the fire. "You getting lonely out there, Ralph? You're welcome to sleep near me and the mice if you like," Tom kidded.

After finishing his meal, Tom added wood to the fire, hoping that some of the chill could be taken out of the lean-to. He led Ralph to a thicket of cedar, loosely tying the lead rope to the branches.

If the mule was attacked by wolves, it would be able to pull the rope loose and flee or fight. Also, if something was to happen to him the animal could eventually free itself and go back to the cabin.

The snow began to fall harder. Tom sat just under the edge of the lean-to and skinned the day's catch. The fire had burned down by the time he finished. He pulled the buffalo coat tighter around his neck to keep out the cold.

The crusted snow around the shelter was two feet-deep. At the rate that it was snowing now, there could easily be another foot by morning. Tom had been using the front wall as a reflector for his fire.

Most nights when he'd slept in the lean-to, he'd left the front open. Tonight, with the heavy snow, he decided that he should pull the front closed. Tom shook the snow off the packs and tossed them into the far end of the shelter.

The wind had started to pick up, blowing the snow sideways. He looked wistfully toward the cedar thicket. He wished that he had a better shelter for the mule.

"Just keep your butt to the wind and I will see you in the morning," he called into the darkness.

Tom rolled some of the rocks that made up the fire pit into his shelter. He could keep his feet warm against them until they cooled. He then took a burning stick from the fire and set it inside the lean-to.

He dragged the closure to the front of the lean-to, backed into it and pulled it as tight as he could. It had been designed to stop animals from entering while they were gone, not for keeping the wind out.

Tom found the tin box that they kept in the shelter for emergencies and opened it. It contained bullets, patches, some black powder, flint, candles, a knife, and a small ball of tinder for starting a fire.

He selected a candle from the box and replaced its cover. He lit the candle by blowing on the glowing brands on the end of the stick. The flickering candlelight did not penetrate the far corners of the shelter.

Locating a spot that was shielded from the

wind, Tom set the candle down. He brushed the snow from his beard and clothing. His frozen breath created clouds in the cramped shelter as he struggled to set up his blankets. Normally he would set them up using the light of the fire.

As fast as Tom brushed the snow off his bedding, the wind would blow more on them through the cracks in the shelter. Finally deciding that the effort was useless, he pulled the blanket over the buffalo skin coat and put the ground cloth over that.

Just before settling down, a gust of wind blew the candle out. "Well, at least the storm saved me from having to snuff out the flame," he muttered, pulling his rabbit skin hat tighter around his ears. Stretching out, he put his feet against the warm stones.

The sound of the mice chewing was the last thing he heard before dozing off. He hoped that they weren't putting holes in his blankets or coat.

The howling of the wind woke Tom. The inside of the lean-to was pitch black. He turned his head to look around and snow fell under the coat collar. In the darkness, it was impossible to tell how much snow had blown into the shelter.

The tall man lay still to prevent more snow from getting in under his covers. He wiggled his toes to make sure that they weren't frozen. His muscles were cramped from lying in one place too long.

With the storm raging outside the lean-to, there was no way to know what time it was. Even if he did know, it would be suicide to venture out of the shelter. For the next several hours he dozed fitfully.

Each time the wind peaked, it would wake him. Tom was forced by his aching body to reposition himself and accept whatever snow found its way in.

Finally, he could lay no longer and sat up.

Feeling around with his unprotected hands, he determined that there were about three inches of snow covering his packs and blankets. He pulled the canteen from under his coat and took a sip of water.

Locating his possible bag, he reached into it and fished out a piece of jerky. With the storm wailing outside, he was unable to hear anything else as he chewed on the dried meat. He suddenly realized that the wind no longer found its way through the hastily constructed walls of the lean-to.

That would mean that the snow had drifted over the shelter. The sound of the storm outside let him know that the snow cover wasn't too deep. The advantage of the drifted snow would be keeping the inside a little warmer.

The next problem came as Tom was finishing up the piece of jerky. He had to relieve himself. The space was small. The only way he could lay down was diagonally. While the packs from the mule weren't large, they still made the cramped space even smaller.

Fumbling around in the dark, he was finally able to accomplish the task. He just hoped that he would remember what part of the lean-to needed to be avoided. Tom took the flint and steel out of his possible bag.

Turning his head so that he wouldn't be blinded, he struck the flint and sent a shower of sparks that lit the shelter momentarily. The inside was covered and coated with windblown snow.

He noticed trails in the snow from the mice he had evicted from the kindling pile. For all he knew, they were now living in his blankets and coat. Sitting in the darkness, Tom thought about the mule braving the elements outside.

All of a sudden, he remembered that the canteen was lying out. Groping around, he located it and put it back under his coat. The cold, leather-covered container only added to his discomfort.

After sitting and listening to the blizzard for what seemed like hours, Tom laid back down. Surprisingly, he did sleep. He dreamed that he was at the barber, getting a haircut.

When he awoke, something had changed. It took a moment to realize what it was. He could no longer hear the storm. He wondered if the snow was so deep that the sound was cut off.

Sitting up, he pushed at the front wall. It didn't budge. Getting to his knees, he put his shoulder against the wall and heaved against the barrier. There was a slight movement.

Snow fell in from the outside. Looking out of the small opening, he could see stars. The blizzard was over! Again, he put his shoulder to the wall and pushed. The snow crunched as it gave way, offering an opening wide enough for Tom to crawl out of.

Finally, out of the dark tomb of the shelter, he stood and stared at the night sky. A sound from behind made him turn. Standing belly deep in the snow was Ralph. Relief flooded over the tall man.

Tom took the trailing halter rope and said, "I may be a fool, old mule, but I think we are going to pack up and head for the cabin."

The snow around the lean-to was too deep to get a fire going and Tom wasn't ready to go back into the small shelter. Pulling the packs out of the lean-to, he pushed the wall closed.

Wading through the hip-deep snow, he

brushed the frozen precipitation from the mule's back and put the packs on. "If the snow is this deep the rest of the way to the cabin, I am going to climb on your back and let you break our trail."

The eastern sky was just starting to show light when the tall man led the animal away from the snow-covered shelter that had kept him safe during the blizzard.

* * *

It was late afternoon when the exhausted man and mule emerged from the trail. The sight of the cabin had never looked better. Smoke was rising from the chimney, promising warmth and the prospect of a hot meal.

Tom stripped the packs and halter from the mule. He put Ralph into the corral with the horses. After pitching some hay to the animal, he picked up the packs and headed into the cabin.

Tom pushed the door open and saw his friend's face break into a smile. Shoving the door shut with his foot, he set the packs down next to it. The welcoming smell of coffee and beans filled his nostrils.

"It has been three days since you left. I worried that the blizzard had caught you away from shelter," Two Buffalo said.

"Three days?" Tom said with surprise. "I was buried by the snow in the lean-to and had no idea how long it had been."

"The side of your face," the chief said.

"What about it?" Tom asked.

"Your beard, there is a round patch that is cut to the skin."

Laughing, Tom rubbed the side of his beard. "One of the damn mice was a barber, I guess."

That night, after some rest and a hot meal, Tom sat in front of the cabin on the split-log bench. It was another clear night and he was drinking coffee while thinking about his wife and son. Had she gotten the letter he had sent with Barnct? He wondered if she was watching the same stars as he was. He observed a star with a long tail. He liked to think that it was a sign from Eva, telling him that everything was okay.

It was March when another storm kept them snowbound for several days. It was not as cold as the February storm, but dropped more snow. The weather finally broke. Tom saddled the roan and took the mule to check the woods trap line. The drifts in front of the cabin were chest-high.

He worried about feed for the horses. That was the main reason he had given the burned-out trapper the pony. If they didn't get a period of fair weather, the haystack would become depleted.

As it was, he was not giving the horses and mule as much as they needed. The tender branches in the fenced corral and around the cabin area had been chewed off as high as the animals could reach.

He chose to ride the long-legged roan because it would be able to bust through the drifts without too much difficulty. As always the mule followed, taking advantage of the trail broken by the lead horse.

Tom stopped for his midday meal near a grove of young aspen trees. The animals took advantage of the forage and chewed on the tender branches and buds. He spent a little extra time to let them eat their fill.

While waiting, he caught sight of a snowshoe

rabbit. Drawing the Colt from under his heavy buffalo skin coat, he dispatched it with a head shot. It would make a fine evening meal.

The trap line had three mink, a marten, and two bobcats. As usual, they were frozen solid and would have to be thawed before he could skin them. Arriving at the drift-covered lean-to, he cleared the snow away from the front and set the front wall across the fire.

Generally he kept his fires small, but to thaw this catch he heaped the wood on and placed them near. Tom rigged a spit and had the rabbit roasting. He had to watch closely to make sure that the branch supporting his meal didn't burn through with the bigger fire.

As the animals thawed enough, Tom began to skin them. The rich, thick fur felt good against his hands. He walked down to the stream to wash the blood off his hands. A late February thaw had opened up parts of the water

He stood on the bank, cleaning his hands in the icy water. All of a sudden, he froze. Within a few inches of his hand was a nice-sized trout. He moved around behind the fish and quickly scooped to try and toss it onto the snow-covered bank.

The startled fish flopped briefly on the snow, trying to get back to the water before stiffening from the cold. Tom knelt, covering the prize with his bare hands. He would enjoy fish for breakfast. He could hardly close his fingers around the fish, due to the cold air on his wet hands.

Slipping, and falling several times, catching himself with his elbows, he climbed the hill back to his camp holding the fish between his numb hands. Tossing it next to his lean-to, he leaned over the fire, holding his hand over the heat. As they warmed, he endured the pins and needles feeling as circulation returned.

Flexing his fingers to regain normal feeling, he took pleasure in the smell of the roasting rabbit. Using his pannikin, he heated water for tea. He sat in the dark, eating the tender rabbit and sipping his tea.

He could hear the roan and mule tear at the evergreen boughs. Next year, he would bring some oats to give to the hard-working animals. He made a silent vow that he would give them plenty once they got back to the fort.

His appetite satisfied and feeling drowsy, he spread his ground tarp and blankets in the lean-to. The fish for breakfast was put inside the shelter to keep it overnight. Kicking off his calf-high moccasins, he crawled into his covers and lay listening to the sounds of the night.

He heard something gnawing. His first thought was that it was a beaver along the stream. Then he realized that it was in his shelter. He smiled, knowing that it was beetles chewing under the bark of the poles on his lean-to. The heat of the fire had awoken them.

The sun was up when Tom stirred under his blankets. Tossing them aside, he pulled on the cold moccasins. He climbed out and added tinder and kindling to the ash on the fire. Blowing on it, he got coals under the ash to glow red. Soon the fire was crackling, warming the area in front of the shelter.

He went to check on the animals. They stood dozing under the evergreens. After relieving himself, he returned to the fire and turned to get the fish from the lean-to. His jaw dropped. It was gone! He saw the tracks of a fisher in the snow near his shelter. During the night, the brave critter had entered the lean-to and had stolen his breakfast!

Packing snow into his pannikin, he set it next to the fire to melt for tea. He reached into his pack and took out some elk jerky. Sitting there, watching the water heat, he chewed on the dried meat. It hardly satisfied him the way a juicy fish would have.

With the meal finished, he closed up the lean-to and started down the second leg of the overland trap line. In one of the foot traps, only a leg of a coyote remained. The rest had been eaten by other coyotes or wolves.

He had seen it before, when animals looking for easy meals followed the trap line and fed on anything that was in the traps. He hoped that this wasn't happening to him. He arrived back at the cabin just before dark.

Two Buffalo sat near the fire pit and had a steaming pot in front of him. Tom called out, "What's for supper?"

Looking up, the old chief smiled. "Tonight we dine well. I found a honey tree and gathered some. I am melting the honey from the comb." He pointed to the Dutch oven. "I used the last of the cornmeal and made a johnnycake. We will have johnnycake with honey."

Tom put the roan and mule into the corral. He returned to the fire pit. "Any coffee?"

"I have a pot staying warm in the fireplace," the chief said.

That night the men split the thick johnnycake and poured the warm honey over it. It made up for the fish that had been taken. The remaining honey was poured into an empty tin to be used in their coffee, or to sweeten cold flour.

The weather stayed fair the rest of March. Each night, the star with the tail would appear in the sky. Tom remembered learning in school that comets looked like large stars and had tails.

Tom was at the trap line lean-to one morning when he awoke to the sound of water dripping. He threw off the covers and it felt warm. It was late March, or early April. In the next couple of weeks they would break camp and head for the fort.

His spirits were high as he headed the roan toward the cabin. This was the last trip to the lean-to, and he had packed the box with emergency supplies on the mule. With the weather warming up, the quality of the furs would rapidly degrade.

Two Buffalo had told him that springs had created open water on some of the ponds and the hungry beaver were venturing out to find tender branches to drag under the ice near their lodges. The chief had put in traps near the openings. The beaver pelts would stay prime longer due to the cold water they swam in.

Tom's thoughts were interrupted when he came across the tracks of three horses crossing his trail. There were also the large tracks of a bear. He swung down from the roan. He examined the tracks the best he could. It looked like the horses were not shod. There were three Crow, maybe Blackfoot, following the bear.

Being several miles from the cabin, Tom figured it was unlikely that the Indians would come back this way and follow his trail. If they succeeded in killing the bear, they would head for their village to sing the song of victory around their fires.

Climbing back on the roan, Tom continued along the trap line. He kept glancing back at the mule to see if it detected any danger. All appeared to be well. Large flakes of snow began to fall.

Suddenly, the mule brayed loudly. Tom turned to look back and never saw the grizzly step out in front of the roan. Before the horse had a chance to move, the bear's large paw swept across the horse's front, ripping open the arteries and knocking the roan over.

Tom flew from the back of the horse, landing several feet away from the trail. The horse went down, kicking violently. Its hoof hit squarely on the joint of the bear's back leg. The grizzly went down while trying to paw and maul the dying horse.

The tall man lay with the wind knocked out of him. He watched as the bear stood growling, guarding its prize. It was unable to put weight on its back leg. The horse lay still in a pool of blood. The mule was gone. It had run back up the trail to safety.

The bear moved away from the horse, sniffing the air. Tom could see his Hawken sticking out from under the downed horse. He knew that he had to get to the rifle. If necessary, he could shoot the bear. The knowledge that it was being followed by hunters made him hope that he did not have to fire the gun and alert them to his presence.

The bear moved a short distance away. Tom crawled to the roan and pulled the Hawken free from the scabbard. He moved back to an aspen windfall, ducking under its snow laden branches, and lay hidden by snow fall on each side.

In a rush, the bear came back to its kill. Unable to stand on its back feet, it raised its head and let out a bone-chilling roar to warn off any predator. The bear then began tearing at the horse's flesh.

Tom was lying upwind of the animal and hoped that it wouldn't catch his scent. After the long hibernation, the grizzly would be hungry. The braves following it might have chased the bear from its den.

The great bear clamped its jaws on the neck of the horse and tried to pull it away from the trail and into some brush. The injured back leg made the task difficult. Tom watched the struggle from under the windfall while the snow continued falling.

At times it was hard to see through the curtain of snow. Suddenly, the large grizzly held its head up, sniffing the air. It smelled something that made it decide to abandon the kill.

Tom remained still, and soon caught sight of three Blackfoot tracking the bear. They stopped at the place where the horse had been killed. He could hear them talking about what had happened.

One of the braves dismounted and squatted down next to the dead animal. There were shouts from another who noticed that the grizzly might have been injured. They talked excitedly for a moment glancing around the area, and then abandoned the kill and continued following the bear.

Lying under the tree, Tom kept the Hawken on the braves until they rode out of sight. The falling snow had made the sign hard to read, and they missed seeing that he had crawled out from under the windfall to get his rifle.

The Blackfoot were carrying older style muzzle-loaders. The guns would be able to kill the grizzly at close range. Tom knew that he had to get out of the area. For one thing, the bear might circle back to feed on the roan. Then again, the Blackfoot might give up on the bear and come looking for the horse's rider.

Pushing the snow aside, Tom crawled out from under the tree. He looked at the snow on his Hawken. There was a good chance that it wouldn't even fire until he warmed and cleaned it. He looked back in the direction that the mule had gone.

He was about a four-hour walk from the cabin. Even now it would be dark when he got back. The mule, Ralph would have to take care of himself. His blanket roll and gear was packed on the mule. His belongings were not worth the risk of wandering in the dark, with an injured bear in the area and the Blackfoot around.

Tom made a large circle around the dead roan before coming back to the trail. He didn't want to leave tracks leading from the animal down the trail. As he walked in the darkening woods, he couldn't shake the feeling that the grizzly was coming up behind him. His back tingled, anticipating the blow of one of the massive paws.

Clumps of fresh snow were falling off the tree branches around Tom. The sounds kept him feeling jumpy. All of a sudden, he knew that he was being followed. He heard the muted footsteps in the snow and the sounds of branches brushing against something moving. Was the bear tracking him? Was it the Blackfoot?

Not trusting the Hawken, he drew the Colt and stepped behind a thick oak tree. He waited. Hardly daring to breathe, he listened. Abruptly, he knew what it was. Ralph was tracking him!

Once the animal caught up to him, Tom

adjusted the pack and climbed onto the mule. He sat, exhausted from his ordeal, as the mule carried him back to the cabin.

Stripping the gear from the mule, he put it into the corral. Two Buffalo heard him ride in and stood in the doorway. He helped Tom bring his gear into the cabin. There was coffee staying warm on the hearth.

Tom told the chief about the grizzly killing the roan and the Blackfoot following the bear. Two Buffalo's eyes shined as he listened to the story.

"You said the bear is injured?" the chief asked. "If we go out in the morning, we may be able to find the grizzly before the Blackfoot. Killing it would be strong medicine."

The tall man looked at his friend. "I could almost smell the breath of that bear. One thing I will not do is go back and try and find it."

"I think I agree with you," Two Buffalo said. "But it would have been something."

* * *

The next two weeks were busy getting ready to go down the mountain. The snow was melting and the ice on the Wind River had broken loose in large sheets. They were back to two pack animals and had to make decisions on what might have to be left behind.

A week before leaving, the traps were pulled from the beaver ponds. The last few pelts they had taken were no longer prime. Tom started moving the furs and skins down from the cave to the cabin. He rolled and folded them to make them pack tighter.

The chief hunted for meat for the trip back to the fort. Most of their supplies were gone. Enjoying a cup of coffee was just a memory. Their cold flour, pemmican and beans were gone. They had eaten the last of their side meat weeks ago. For some time it had been rabbits or beaver, seasoned with salt.

That evening, the chief came back with a small doe. After a meal of venison, the rest would have to be made into jerky for the trip. The men set several snares around the cabin and caught enough rabbits to keep from starving.

They brought the horses and mule to the meadows and let them graze on the brown grass. Once in a while they would find some green grass growing in an area that got full sun.

On a drizzly, gray morning, the men decided that it was time to head down toward the fort. The furs and skins were packed along with gear that they wanted to take with them. The remaining items were cached in the cave. They had enough food to make the trip. It was time to leave.

CHAPTER TWELVE

The Wind River tumbled over its banks while the men rode east toward the fort. Tom wondered if it was still Fort William, or had the name changed to Fort John? He thought about his family. He would close his eyes and envision Eva's face. He knew that little Isaac would be much bigger than when he'd left. He planned to spend time getting to know his son.

Crossing the streams and creeks flowing into the Wind River were more of a challenge than before. The snow melting at the higher elevations filled them to flood level.

The men's progress was slow. After the first night on the road, they came to a wide granite ledge that had water seeping from the cliff above. During the frigid night the ledge became covered with a sheet of ice.

They scared up a young button buck that ran ahead of them onto the ledge. Its feet went out from under, and the animal fell. It fought to regain its footing, without success. Soon, the thrashing deer slid over the edge of the ledge and into the raging river.

The men sat watching, unable to help the struggling animal as it was being swept down the river, swimming for its life. Finally, it got a foothold on some boulders near the shore and hung there, gasping for breath.

"I don't want to follow that deer into the river," Tom said. "We best look for a way around the ledge, or sit tight until the sun melts the ice."

"We will have to find another way. It will be late afternoon before the sun will reach the ledge and then it may not be warm enough to melt it," the chief figured.

It took most of the day to backtrack and find a way around the ledge. When they finally got back to the river, it was only a couple of miles downstream from the sheet of ice.

As darkness set in, the chief put up his hand. "I smell smoke. It comes from the north."

"That would put whoever has the fire on the other side of the river," Tom said. "We may as well camp here for the night. If those across the river are bad guys, they can't get across to hurt us."

The spot turned out to be a good one. There was new grass for the horses, and a ridge that offered shelter from prying eyes and the wind. Tom stripped the gear from the horses and pack animals while Two Buffalo put together a small fire.

"I saw some cattails near an old beaver dam just off the river. The roots will make a fine meal," the chief said. Taking a poke bag from the packs, and his bow, he headed out into the darkness.

"You going to shoot the roots?" Tom called after him.

Tom knew better, though. In the wilds, a man never traveled without a weapon to defend himself or bag unexpected game.

The night air was cold and damp. The tall man moved closer to the fire, hoping that they didn't get more rain. It could even end up being snow coming in on the north wind. He set their pannikins next to the fire to heat up. Earlier, the chief had picked some spring flowers that would make a decent tea.

Tom moved away from the fire when he caught the sound of a branch against clothing. He was sure that it was Two Buffalo returning, but in the mountains it was best to be watchful.

He heard the chief say, "We eat well tonight. There was a muskrat swimming near the bank."

While Two Buffalo skinned the rat, Tom packed clay around the cattail roots and pushed them into the coals of the fire. An hour later, the two men sat enjoying their meal. The flowers made an excellent tea to top off the night.

Shortly after sunrise, the two riders and their pack animals left the protection of the ridge. It had not rained or snowed during the night, but the cold north wind would make it an uncomfortable day.

They caught sight of the campfire that they had smelled the night before. Three trappers were huddled around a fire on the far side of the river. They had put up a makeshift shelter to keep the weather off.

The trappers would have to wait for the Wind River to go down before they could chance crossing it. The only other option was to ride north to the Bighorn and look for a place to cross there.

As they passed, the two parties yelled their greeting across the violent water. One of the men shouted, "Save us some of that rye when you get to the Laramie."

Tom could see some fair-sized packs near their horses, so it appeared that the men had had a good winter. It took one more day before the two men left the Wind River and cut across towards the North Platte River.

Spring in the lower elevations was well ahead of the mountain range. Wild flowers added color to the rolling plains. Young green grass was sprouting, offering better feed for their underfed stock. The rough winter coats on the animals would soon start to shed.

The men could spend hours with a curry comb, removing the winter coat and debris that had imbedded in the hair. Tom knew that some men just let the hair fall out with time. But this could take months, and when the weather got warmer the horses could become overheated.

Shortly after reaching the North Platte River, the men came across an encampment of soldiers. They had a chance to enjoy coffee after a long spell without it. Some of the soldiers fancied getting a mink fur to take back to a favorite gal. The two trappers were able to trade for a few items that would make the next couple of weeks of travel more pleasant.

They did find out that the fort was now called Fort John. They were also warned about a group of renegade Crow who were raiding emigrants and trappers. They were led by Red Wolf.

The name was familiar to the trappers, and Tom told the soldiers of the run-in they'd had with the band while hunting buffalo.

The men continued down the south side of the

river. The Platte meandered as it worked its way to join with the Laramie River. In some cases, Tom and Two Buffalo would ride across country to save miles.

A day's travel from the fort, they spent the night on the banks of a clear stream flowing into the North Platte River. Tom caught several trout for their evening meal. They had gotten some flour and side meat from the soldiers. Tom mixed a little salt into the flour and dusted the fish. He then fried them in the grease from the side meat. The nicely browned trout were a meal to remember.

Tom was anxious to get going in the morning and had their gear and packs on the animals before they ate their morning meal. While the chief acted like he was in no hurry, the smile on his face said otherwise.

The men carried their rifles across the saddles as they rode toward the fort. They were watchful of other travelers. The packs of furs could offer quick money for those too lazy to spend the winter in the mountains.

It was late afternoon when the fort came into sight. Tom was surprised to see that much of the stockade had been torn down. They could see workers building the new fort on a bluff overlooking the Laramie River.

They found Louie busy in his trading post. His face lit up when he saw the trappers. "Tom! Two Buffalo! Welcome back from the mountains."

He poured them some coffee from the potbelly stove and set a bottle of rye next to their cups. "This bottle is on me," he said.

The chief declined the rye in his coffee, but Tom poured in a good measure. Taking a sip of doctored coffee, Tom asked, "Have you heard from

Eva?"

"Not since I sent your letter to her. Chess is around, and I planned to ask him to bring a few things to her," the proprietor said.

"Is Chess getting around well?" Tom asked.

"He is as good as new. I hear he has partnered up with another hunter. They will be supplying meat for the army," Louie said, walking to the low doorway and looking at their pack animals. "Bring your furs in and let's have a look."

The rest of the day was spent tallying up the value of the furs and skins. By the time they finished, Tom had enjoyed several shots of rye and was ready to call it a night. Louie sent a boy out to take their stock to the livery and give them a good portion of oats.

Tom spent the night in a back room of the trading post while the chief chose to sleep outdoors, away from the smells of the fort. Light coming in from a fly-specked window awoke the tall man.

His mouth was dry and his head throbbed. "Damn rye," he muttered as he struggled to get his boots on.

He walked into the main room and found Two Buffalo, clear-eyed and drinking coffee. "The evil spirits in the bottle can cloud a man's mind," the chief warned him.

"It doesn't do much good for the stomach either," Tom said.

After a big bowl of porridge sweetened with maple syrup, and several cups of coffee, the tall man was ready to face the day.

Both trappers were pleased with the amount offered by Louie for the furs. The beaver pelts were only a fraction of what they had been a few years ago, but the two men had expected as much. They agreed to give a portion to Chess. He had been wounded defending the last venture and it had caused him to miss the winter trapping.

After selecting several items to bring to Eva, they settled up with Louie and went to get their horses. They paid the hostler for the night's stay in the livery, then headed out for the cabin that Tom had built for his young family.

Tom galloped the last mile to the cabin. Two Buffalo took over leading the pack horses. As Tom approached, he saw that the cabin door was open. The corral was empty and the gate poles were down.

His first feeling was disappointment, because it appeared that they had gone away for the day. Once home, Tom didn't want to spend a single extra minute away from his family.

As he got close to the cabin, he caught his breath. Someone was lying just outside the door. As he rode up, he could see that it was the young brave that had wintered with Eva. He had been scalped!

Jumping off the horse, he stumbled to the doorway. "Eva! Eva, where are you?" Tom shouted. The cabin was empty.

Two Buffalo rode up to the cabin. His face was without expression as he swung down from the paint and knelt next to his dead nephew.

Tom stood in the doorway, with his hand on the jamb, to prevent his shaky legs giving way. The inside of the cabin had been gone through. What was left lay scattered on the floor.

Two Buffalo rose from his nephew and stood beside his shaken friend. "I must take the boy to his family for burial. When I return, we will go and take vengeance on the ones that did this."

"It is my fault," Tom said, fighting back the tears. "I should have come here last night instead of getting drunk."

"What happened here happened two, maybe three days ago," the chief said softly. "It is not too late. When I come back, we will go find your family and kill those that took them."

"My wife and son may be dead already," Tom said. "And . . . your nephew's wife."

"If they wanted to kill them, we would have found their bodies here at the cabin. They have been taken for other purposes," Two Buffalo assured his friend.

Tom sat on the bench in front of the cabin, unable to move as he watched the chief put his nephew on the pack horse. He took a couple of items and stuck them into the bedroll behind his saddle.

Two Buffalo mounted the paint and looked at his friend. "You must accept what has happened and clear your mind to the task in front of us. If you cannot do this, soon I will be standing beside your grave."

Tom watched his friend ride away to bring his nephew to the Cheyenne village. The chief wasn't even out of sight before the dam of tears broke and Tom wept like a child. For the second time, Eva had been taken from him. He feared that this time he would not have the strength needed to bring her back.

It was dark before Tom was able to put up the dun and mule. He hadn't eaten since morning. He felt drained of the will to go on. When his brother had been killed on the Ohio River, he'd thought that it was the worst feeling that he would ever have.

Now he knew that he'd been wrong. The

thought of losing his wife and son created an ache inside that could not even be expressed. He sat in front of the cabin, looking at the sky. He didn't have the will to spend the night inside.

He sat, surrounded by the sounds of the night, and heard none of it. It was as though the world around him was gone. He played the chief's words over and over in his thoughts.

"I must accept what has happened? How?" Tom whispered.

Then, he shouted at the darkness, "How! How can I?"

Finally, sleep came. Troubled, unsatisfying sleep, and without peace, but it came.

CHAPTER THIRTEEN

It was still dark when Tom opened his eyes. He was cold, and covered with dew. Suddenly, his mind was clear. All of the lessons that Tom had learned from those he'd been mentored by in the past ran through his mind.

He realized that he was not helpless. There was much that he could do, and do it now. To sit and do nothing, while fearing the worst, does no man any good. If, at some point, he finds that his family is lost to him, then that is the time to start grieving. Until that time, he must believe that they are alive and he will again be with them.

Getting up from the bench, Tom walked down to the pond. He stripped off his clothes in the cold night air and bathed. The cool spring water sharpened his senses. Walking back to the cabin, naked as the day he was born, he experienced a surge of hope.

"I will find them and bring my family back," he vowed.

Daylight found him dressed in clean clothes,

making his breakfast over the fire pit in the front yard. He must be ready for what was to come. He must eat and sleep. A time would come when he would meet those who had done this, so he had to remain strong.

There was much to do before Two Buffalo returned. Tom began to read the sign around the cabin. He found where the attackers had waited and watched the cabin. It appeared that they had visited the spot several times.

He memorized the tracks around the cabin. Painstakingly, he worked out the events of the attack. In the shambles of the cabin, he determined that Eva had just started the morning meal. It had come in the morning.

The nephew had probably been surprised when stepping outside. There was no sign of blood inside the cabin. The women and the baby had been taken from the cabin before it was searched for anything valuable.

He found an area where they had been held. In the dust he saw *R V*. He got up and headed back toward the cabin. Abruptly, he stopped and went back to where he had noticed the letters.

One leg of the letter V was too short. It was possible that the person writing the letters had been pulled away. The V could have been an L or . . . W. Red Wolf! While he could be wrong, Tom was confident that Eva had tried to leave a message for him.

When Two Buffalo returned from bringing his nephew home for burial, Tom was ready. To keep busy while going over what he had found, he had straightened the cabin. Tom had brushed the dun and mule. His saddlebags were packed. Most importantly, his weapons were cleaned and loaded.

The chief looked at his friend with approval. "We are ready to go get your family and my nephew's wife."

"Eva left a message," Tom informed the chief. "I believe she wrote *R W* in the dust. Red Wolf and the other Crow renegades did this."

"They had watched the cabin from above," Two Buffalo said, pointing to a rise beyond the cabin. "They attacked when the sun came up. My nephew was surprised when he left the cabin."

"I agree. But how would you know?" Tom asked.

"I read the sign when we got here. When I left, I rode around the cabin and found the spot where they watched," the chief explained. "Their sign I had seen before on the plain where we hunted. Yes, it was Red Wolf. He is riding with four warriors."

"I followed the tracks for a while when bringing my nephew. They were riding toward the North Platte River. I did find out their own tribe has shunned them. They are welcome at no one's teepee," the chief finished.

"They are days ahead of us. Could we have passed them?" Tom wondered.

Two Buffalo shook his head no. "It would take two days to reach the river from here. We wouldn't have seen them. It is feared that they plan to go north along the Powder River and ask the Lakota to join them and fight the white man."

"They can ride to the gates of Hell and ask the devil to join them. I am ready to follow and fight them," Tom bristled.

Listening without comment, Two Buffalo liked

his friend's determination, as long as Tom didn't become reckless when pursuing the Crow. Driven by anger, a man might ignore warnings and run into a trap. He saw that his friend was ready to travel. The chief had everything he needed on the paint.

Two Buffalo had left his pack horse with the Cheyenne. He questioned Tom about bringing the mule with him.

"Ralph here helped me bring Eva back the first time. I wouldn't think of leaving him behind," Tom said confidently.

"I believe you're right," the chief said.

The two men left the cabin in search of the captives. Before leaving, Tom had put tinder and wood into the fireplace for cooking. Everything had been put away, just waiting for Eva's return. He had packed a new dress and a toy in his saddlebags that he'd gotten for his family. When they were rescued, he would give the gifts to them.

The captives had been taken in the direction of the Powder River basin. It would be a two-week trip, maybe more. Once the Crow got to the area, there were a number of valleys and canyons that they could hide in. It would be almost impossible to find them.

Upon leaving the cabin, the trail was quickly picked up. The weather had been favorable, leaving the tracks easy to follow. The sky was clear and the day warm. Tom wore his flat-brimmed hat and buckskins. His possible bag hung at his side with extra powder, bullets, and other odds and ends that he might need.

The Colt was on his right side and a Bowie knife was on the left. The Hawken rifle was in the new scabbard that he had gotten at Louie's, replacing the one that had been lost when the roan was attacked.

Two Buffalo sat straight on the paint. He had new buckskins that were given to him by the Cheyenne. He had a round-topped hat with a brim that drooped a bit. He wore a medicine bag on a string around his neck. He said that it helped him look into the future.

The chief carried a bow and quiver of arrows across the back of his saddle. Across the front he carried the Kentucky Long Rifle. He wore a skinning knife at his side and a possible bag over his shoulder.

Riding toward the northwest, Tom said, "If we pass anyone going to the fort, we should send word about Red Wolf."

"It has been done," the chief replied. "A brave in the Cheyenne village trades with Louie. He will bring word to him. Then Louie can let the army know."

"Good," Tom said. "I thank you for doing that."

It was the first of May. The trees were budding and wild flowers of yellow, blue, and red were everywhere. Given different circumstances, just being out here would be a pleasure. The tall man hoped that he could enjoy the area with his family in the coming years.

He no longer felt the emotion that had beset him when he'd found his family gone. He was confident that they would be successful getting them back. The tracks that they were following showed that the renegade party was not running.

The Crow had stopped and made camp less than a day's ride from the cabin. It was in a wide-open area next to a small grove of cottonwoods. They had killed the pony and used it for food. The captives were kept tied, except for little Isaac. Tom could see where he had been walking around the camp, free to roam.

Two Buffalo saw Tom looking at his son's prints. "When war parties raided and took prisoners, they would kill those that could slow them down. Eva would have encouraged the young boy to be nice to the captors, hoping that the braves would like the boy, and keep him with his mother, rather than leaving him to starve on the plains."

"Why did they take the women and not your nephew?" Tom asked. Two Buffalo stared straight ahead, not answering his friend.

Tom realized that it was a stupid question. Eva and the young Cheyenne girl had been taken by Red Wolf to be slaves or wives for his braves. Eventually, they would be expected to join them in their blankets. If the women refused they could be beaten, or worse.

He fought to force the thought out of his mind. Once again, he would face what happened when they got back together. To torture himself with these thoughts now would do him no good.

Tom and Two Buffalo spent the night in the cottonwood grove. They woke the next morning to heavy, low cloud cover. They ate jerky and drank water for their morning meal before continuing on the Crow's trail.

By late morning it began to rain. The storm came with a strong west wind that caused a sideways rain. The men rode toward a stand of aspen, hoping to gain some protection from the wetness and even more from the wind. They huddled under their ground tarps and watched the deluge around them.

The violent storm ended in just over an hour.

Their gear and their blankets were soaked. They hung the wet blankets and clothes over the aspen branches. Tom got a fire going to make coffee while the gear and clothing dried.

By afternoon they were back on their way. The tracks that they had been following were all but washed out. Two Buffalo looked to the north. "The Crow have been heading along the Platte River. We will continue until we find tracks, or maybe a place they spent the night."

Tom sat on the dun, looking at the hills and ridges along the river. "If they are heading toward the Powder River, they will stay along the Platte until it turns to southwest. The Crow will then have to head north to pick up the south fork of the Powder. My guess is they will spend a day or two on the Platte before heading north. That camp should give us plenty of sign."

He stated this with a lot more confidence than he felt. Tom knew that they had to try and think like Red Wolf and the Crow. Patterns had started to emerge as they followed the trail.

The Crow had not been traveling long, or fast. It could be that they didn't fear pursuit. Their campsites were easily identified. The men slept away from their captives. One man would watch them.

Tom urged the dun on. Ralph followed the other horses without the need of a halter. The chief rode alongside Tom, his eyes on the horizon.

The tall man began to question the months that he had been gone. Had his longing to be a mountain man been stronger than the desire to be with his family? If he had stayed, he could have protected Eva and Isaac.

Deep in thought, he missed hearing what Two Buffalo had said. "I'm sorry, I . . . what did you say?"

"They are not running," the chief repeated.

"That's because they don't think anyone knows what they did," Tom pointed out. "And, they are several days ahead of us."

The chief did not acknowledge the last comment and fell into silence. The men moved apart to cover more ground. They were looking for six people on horseback, who would likely make a lasting mark on the sparse ground cover.

CHAPTER FOURTEEN

Eva lay under a ledge, covered by a thin blanket, holding Isaac close to her. She could hear the snores of her captors a short distance away. The stress of the past several days had left her exhausted, yet unable to sleep.

She squeezed her eyes closed and pictured her husband with his curly brown hair and broad shoulders, the way his muscles rippled when he worked. She thought about the pain she'd felt watching him ride away last fall to follow his dream, and the loneliness of being so far from the one she loved.

Her mind wandered back. The winter had been long. Having the other couple living with her in the small cabin had given her company, but she had missed having Tom hold her. She'd worried that he might get hurt on the Wind River. The long winter months of being cooped up in the cabin had given her far too much time to worry.

Her one joy was Isaac. He was a happy baby,

waking with a smile that stayed on his face all day. He'd been able to crawl around the dirt floor of the cabin. Tried as she had to keep him on the buffalo skin rug, he'd seemed to be happiest on the bare earth.

It had been the end of March when Chess had brought some supplies sent by Louie and a letter from Tom. The last thing Eva had expected was word from her husband. Chess had told her that Tom and Two Buffalo had helped the man out after his cabin had burnt. Tom had asked him to carry the letter back to her.

Eva had wished that she could have talked with the man. She would have had so many things to ask him. She kept the letter on her after that. She had never received a letter before. It had been short, but he'd said that he missed her and that he was safe. He had promised to come back as soon as the passes melted.

Chess had taken the buckskin back with him and had thanked Eva for taking care of it over the winter. She'd stood in the doorway and watched their friend and hunting partner ride away, glad that he had healed from his wounds.

Each evening, Eva had sat near the fireplace and traced the words that Tom had written to her. Doing so had made her feel closer to him. Tahkeome and Lona had kidded her while she re-read the letter.

As it had started to get colder, Eva would have the baby sleep with her. His cooing and squirming had made her feel happy. At night, when she'd been nursing the baby, she would whisper stories about Tom to the boy.

Tahkeome had come back into the cabin, stomping the snow off his moccasins. "It is cold

156

tonight. The sky is clear and tomorrow should be sunny. I will go on the ridge and see if there is anything to hunt."

Lona had put some more wood onto the fire. Sparks had flown up the chimney as she had arranged the fresh fuel. Eva had sat next to the fireplace and taken out the letter. Tahkeome had taken his wife's hand. She'd giggled as he led her towards their blankets.

* * *

Two weeks later, Tahkeome had come back from hunting and talked of tracks in the woods above the cabin. Whoever it was had come to the place many times.

"Do you think they are white men?" Eva had asked.

"No," Tahkeome had answered. "They aren't Cheyenne either, maybe Crow. They could be hunting. The deer have a trail near there."

Lona had filled a bowl of soup for her husband. The conversation had drifted away from the tracks in the woods.

The snow had been melting fast. Soon, flowers would be blooming across the grassy plains. Eva had felt excitement, knowing that in the next couple of weeks Tom would return from the mountains.

She would put Isaac into the cradleboard and take him for walks out on the plain. One day, she had been coming back through the pines and she'd heard a horse galloping away. She had found the place that Tahkeome had spoken of. Someone had been there, and ridden away when she'd come though the pines.

Looking at the young boy in the cradleboard, she'd said, "When your father comes home, he will take care of whoever is coming to this spot."

Eva had found an area near the cabin for a garden. As soon as it got a little warmer, she'd planned to start digging it up. Tom had told her stories about the wonderful vegetables that his family had grown in a place called Vermont.

With winter almost over, the Cheyenne couple had been getting anxious to head back to their village. Eva had been thinking about going to the fort to wait for Tom and Two Buffalo to return.

"If you want," she'd told the couple, "I can go to the fort and you can go back to your village. I can leave any time now."

The evening had been one of excitement and planning. Eva had begun sorting items that she would need at the fort. Lona had started placing their stuff near the door, readying them to be packed onto the horses.

That night, Eva had gone to bed happy, knowing that she would see Tom a day or two sooner by meeting him at the fort. She'd also wanted to thank Louie for sending supplies to her. She had dreamed about seeing Tom at the fort that night. She'd kept trying to get near him, but people wouldn't let her get by.

She'd awoken, frustrated from the dream. Hurrying out of bed, Eva had gone to the fireplace to start the morning fire. She had then set a pot of water to heat and had hurried back to the warmth of her bed.

She had heard Tahkeome stirring. She'd watched him sit up and cough. He'd then broken wind, a habit that left the air in the cabin foul each morning.

He had always told her that it was the cooking. She had been glad that he would be going back to the Cheyenne village in the next day or so.

He'd gotten up and headed for the door to go relieve himself. Pulling it open, he had stood looking out on the plain. "Today will be a good day for hunting," he'd said.

With that, he had stepped out, there had been the sound of a gunshot and Tahkeome had collapsed onto the ground. A second later, the huge form of a man had filled the doorway. What had happened the next few minutes was a blur.

Lona had screamed at the sight of her husband's shooting. She'd shrunk back and had covered her naked body with the blanket as the man had entered the room. Eva, in a loose house dress, had picked up Isaac and had held him close to her. She had recognized the ragged scar on the left cheek. It was Red Wolf!

The Crow leader had been followed into the room by three other braves. They had begun to reach and grab for everything, throwing what they hadn't wanted onto the floor. The women had sat, not daring to move.

Tom had told Eva to keep the long rifle loaded and near her bed. Tahkeome had used it to hunt and had taken it over. It had leaned against the wall near the door, out of her reach. She hadn't even been sure if it had been loaded.

The Mackinaw gun was in the small room, also empty. Eva had kept a small knife by the side of the bed and had hid it in the cradleboard while the cabin was ransacked.

In the next few minutes, the women had

expected to be raped, killed and scalped. There had also been the chance they could be taken as captives for the pleasure of these men later.

Eva's other fear had been for little Isaac. She'd heard of babies being picked up and smashed against the wall. Then, sometimes, they'd been left alone to wander on the plain, ending up as prey for the wolves and coyotes.

She'd held the cradleboard and had decided that if they reached for Isaac, she would plunge the knife into the man trying to get the baby. Then she would send little Isaac to the other side. She would not let them brutalize her child.

Red Wolf had stood in the middle of the room. Satisfied that all valuables had been found, he had sent the men outside. Turning to Eva, he had motioned her to go out. Holding the baby close, she had moved to the door.

Next, he'd pushed the crying Lona with his foot. She'd started to scream and he had struck her with the back of his hand. Grabbing her by the hair, he had dragged her outside of the cabin. Eva had stood looking at the body of Tahkeome. They had scalped and mutilated him.

Lona had lain crying, her back to her dead husband. Eva had sat in the dust, holding the baby. While the Crow had been busy looking at what they had found, she'd scratched R W into the dust.

Barely finished, the scowling leader had grabbed Eva and shoved her toward the others. Eva had struggled to hold on to her child as she stumbled forward.

Two of the braves had brought the horses from the corral. Red Wolf had led one of the mustangs to Eva. Pushing her towards it, the leader had taken hold of her and had lifted her onto the horse. Eva had sat holding the baby in the cradleboard close to her.

The braves had then grabbed the naked Lona and had placed her on the second mustang. Huddled on the horse, she had crouched forward and had held the mane with both fists, shaking with sobs. They'd put the things taken from the cabin on the pony.

Red Wolf had led the group away from the cabin. Eva had clung to the horse, expecting the Crow to leave at a gallop. Instead, they had trotted the horses west toward the North Platte River. Two of the younger braves had brought up the rear, making sure that the women couldn't get away.

Eva had looked down at her child, and she'd whispered, "I will die before I let them hurt you."

They had ridden until midday. When they'd reached a small stream, Red Wolf and his braves dismounted. Eva had slid from the mustang and knelt near the water to drink. Lona had hesitated to get down and one of the young braves had grabbed her and thrown her into the water. She'd splashed in the shallow stream, water washing over her nakedness.

Eva had then gone to the pack on the pony. She'd reached in and dug out a buckskin sack dress. Shifting the cradleboard to her back, she had walked into the water and helped Lona to the shore. She had glanced at Red Wolf, who sat watching her.

Feeling more confident because he had not reacted to what she had done, Eva had pulled the buckskin dress over Lona's naked, trembling body. Standing close to her, Eva had hissed, "If you keep acting this way, they will have their way with you and leave you dead on the plain. You will have a lifetime to cry for Tahkeome. Now is not the time."

After a short break at the stream, Red Wolf had led the group on. Lona had quit crying and had sat expressionless on the mustang. Eva had nursed the baby while they rode. She had had no food since the night before and felt the burn of hunger in her stomach.

Both women had been barefoot and had ridden without saddles on the mustangs. It had been tiring, hanging onto the round-bellied animals. When the group had stopped near a grove of cottonwood, the braves had set up camp. Eva had looked at the position of the sun and had wondered, *Why would Red Wolf stop this early?*

One of the braves had tied Lona, hand and foot, next to the trees. Eva had been left untied, to take care of Isaac. The brave had motioned that he would kill Lona if Eva tried to get away.

The women were startled when they had heard the screams of the pony. They had watched as it had staggered, blood streaming from its throat. The Crow had killed the horse for food. Laughing and kidding, the men had sat around a fire, roasting strips of horse flesh. After they had eaten for a while, one of the braves had brought the animal's liver for them.

Isaac had become impatient to get out of the cradleboard. Eva had set him onto the ground, and had taken the liver over to the men's fire. Picking up one of the roasting sticks, she'd held the meat over the flames.

After browning the liver on all sides, she'd then walked back to the tree. Placing the meat on a log, she had looked at Red Wolf. She'd indicated that she needed a knife. The leader had nodded to one of his braves, who had handed her his rusted knife.

Eva had cut the liver up, as best she could. She'd handed some of the nearly raw meat to Lona. She had been thankful that the grieving woman was willing to eat. The horse's liver had made a satisfying meal. Normally, the braves would have eaten the liver first. She'd guessed that Red Wolf had sent it over to her because she had been nursing a child.

Once the liver had been cut up, the Crow had taken his knife back. The braves had seemed to enjoy the playfulness of Isaac, so Eva had let him wander around the camp. She'd kept the cradleboard close, which held her hidden knife. While the baby had crawled around playing, Eva had never taken her eyes off him.

Lona had chewed on the meat, bloody juice running down her chin and dripping onto the buckskin dress. Eva had noticed some swelling and bruising next to her left eye from Red Wolf's blow.

"We must eat whatever they offer, and give them no reason to leave us behind," Eva had cautioned Lona.

"You mean leave us dead," Lona had corrected her. After a short pause, she'd continued. "I am with child. Maybe two months." Tears had welled in her eyes.

"Then it is even more important that you live. Tahkeome's child, maybe a son, grows inside you," Eva had told her.

Eva had watched as the braves continued to gorge themselves with meat. Red Wolf had sat to the side, eating sparingly of the horse. His dark eyes had been fixed on the women, noticing every move they made.

There had been a small pool of water near the far edge of the cottonwood. Little Isaac had gotten covered with dirt from playing around the camp. One of the braves had let him suck on a piece of meat. Grabbing it, the baby had crawled, dragging it in the dirt as he'd headed back towards his mother.

Climbing onto his mother's legs, he'd offered her a taste of the sand-covered meat. Smiling at her small son, Eva had taken the meat from the child. He had needed to be bathed before being put to bed.

Eva had stood and pointed to the water. "I need to bathe the boy."

She'd stared at the leader, waiting for him to acknowledge her request. Red Wolf had given a short command to one of the braves. Unhappy at being sent away from the feast, he'd walked over and shoved her in the direction of the pool.

As darkness had come to the plain, the braves had spread out their sleeping skins or blankets, and laid on their backs with extended bellies filled from the pony meat. Eve and Lona had huddled together, trying to keep warm as the heat from the high desert plain had been quickly lost.

The Crow leader had sat at the edge of the camp, watching the back trail. After several hours, he'd returned to the camp and dug into the items gotten from the cabin. He'd walked over to the shivering women and had tossed two blankets at their feet.

The captives had wrapped themselves in the covers and were finally able to sleep. Eva had held Isaac close to her and prayed to her husband's god that he would watch over them.

The next morning had been filled with the sounds of the braves groaning and trying to void themselves of the meal that they'd had the night before. Sometime during the night, Red Wolf had woken one of the other braves to keep watch over the women and back trail.

The leader had brought Eva to the partially butchered horse. He'd handed her a skinning knife and told her to cut up the remaining meat. As soon as the sun had come up, flies were attracted to the carcass. The braves had done a wasteful job of cutting the meat.

Eva had skinned a good-sized piece of the hide from the horse. Spreading it on the dirt, she'd removed as much useable meat as possible. Soon, she'd had a sizeable pile ready to take with them. Pulling the ends of the horse hide over the meat, she'd cut sinew from the legs of the animal and had tied the bundle together.

Much useable meat had been left on the carcass. They'd had no way to carry more of the animal. Breaking camp, the braves had loaded the goods and meat onto one of the mustangs. The two women and Isaac had ridden the other.

When passing a rocky area near the river, two of the younger braves had broken off and ridden toward the outcrop. They'd dug into the bag of meat and left with handfuls for their meal.

The group had continued in a westerly direction until they'd arrived at a canyon that opened a short distance away from the river and ran about a quarter-mile long. The walls were steep, and had made it easier for the Crow to watch their captives. The cook fire would be well-hidden, and they had an area of high ground to watch for anyone coming from the east.

Eva had noticed that the area had been used before. The canyon floor was littered with bones from game. A large stack of wood had been brought in. The area around the cook fire was worn, and had blackened from many uses.

The women had been put under the overhanging ledge. They had been allowed to keep the blankets, and were given additional clothing from the pack gotten at the cabin. Lona had not been tied, unlike the prior stops. One of the braves had started to give her extra attention. She'd tried to keep her distance without outwardly rejecting him.

* * *

Eva continued to toss and turn as she thought of the events that had brought them to this canyon. The sound of one of the braves throwing wood into the fire pit jarred her awake. Without realizing it, Eva had finally drifted off to sleep in the wee hours of the morning.

Looking out from under the ledge, she saw the heavy cloud cover. A breeze brought the fresh smell of rain. After two days of heat in the canyon, the rain would be a welcome change.

The rain came shortly after the morning meal. They were hit with a severe storm that filled the rocky floor with running water. The ground under the ledge was raised and kept the water from the women. The braves had been camped closer to the mouth of the canyon. When the rain came they moved to a protected area on the west side.

The duration of the rain was short. Red Wolf was upset after it ended. He walked back and forth across the canyon floor, shaking his fist and shouting.

Lona cowered near Eva. "He is angry because of the rain. The hard rain will wash out our tracks."

Eva looked at her friend with surprise. "You understand Crow?"

"Some. We had a Crow woman living in our village," Lona explained.

Picking Isaac up, Eva walked out from under the ledge. She wondered why having the tracks washed out should bother Red Wolf. That would protect them from being found . . . .

Suddenly, she realized that he wanted to be followed! He wanted Tom to follow him. Eva felt her heart pounding under the thin gingham dress. Somehow, the Crow had learned that her husband and Two Buffalo were back from the mountains.

They planned to ambush them when the unsuspecting men came riding to save her. Tom and Two Buffalo would assume whoever took her would continue running. Then it turned out that the severe storm could ruin their scheme to draw the quarry in. Somehow she would have to find a way to escape and warn her husband.

* * *

Less than a day's ride from the canyon, unknown to Eva, the men whom she hoped to warn rode slowly, looking for the trail lost after the rain.

The sun was low in the western sky when Two Buffalo stopped and waved Tom over. Urging the dun to a trot, he joined the chief.

"The tracks of two riders," Two Buffalo said, pointing to the disturbed ground.

"Two?" Tom questioned. "We are looking for six, maybe more."

Pointing to an outcropping of rock near the

river, Two Buffalo said, "They came from up there."

The chief swung down and inspected the tracks. Looking up at his friend, he said, "Follow the tracks back to the rocks. Let me know what you find."

Two Buffalo walked, leading the paint in the direction in which the riders had gone. Tom went to check out the outcrop. He found the place where the riders had waited. The rock structure rose above the rest of the area, offering a view for miles around

Tom swung off his horse and tied it to some scrub brush. Walking around the area, he found evidence that the location had been used for several days. Whoever the occupants were had tied their horses in a wash just west of the outcrop.

Meals had been cooked over a small fire. Some of the charred wood had been washed away by the rain storm. Another fire had been lit after the storm. Those who had stayed there had worn moccasins, and there were marks on the sandstone rock where they had climbed to gain higher vantage.

Tom placed his foot in the stirrup and swung back onto the dun. He could see the mule chewing on the vegetation near the point where they had found the tracks. The chief was riding toward the rocky outcrop. Tom rode to meet Two Buffalo, anxious to tell his friend what he had found.

Tom described the camp and the estimated time it had been occupied while they rode back toward the outcrop. The chief thought over the information.

Two Buffalo concluded, "I believe Red Wolf used this to watch for us. He took Eva and your son, knowing we would come after them." Two Buffalo pointed past the outcrop. "Look across the river."

Tom looked at the far bank and the plain

beyond.

Two Buffalo continued, "From here they could have seen us returning from the Wind River. It is only one day's hard ride to get back to the cabin area to let Red Wolf know of our return. Then they had the two riders wait here to watch for us coming after them."

"Why would he do all this?" Tom asked. "He could have attacked and killed us on the trail to the fort. Red Wolf would have had our scalps and our winter's catch."

"Red Wolf needs followers," the chief explained. "He has to kill us to gain back respect lost when we defeated him on the plains. The taking of your family before killing you will increase your pain and strengthen his medicine."

Tom looked at their back trail again, and then across the river. "Maybe to Red Wolf it makes sense." Shaking his head, he continued, "To me it doesn't."

Darkness was settling in and the lookout location was a protected place to spend the night. They picketed the horses and mule near some brown grass, and then built a small fire to make their meal.

Tom sat in the dark, finishing his coffee. He stared in the direction in which the lookouts had ridden. There was no light of a fire, nor did he expect to see one. On the far side of the river he caught sight of a large cook fire from some trappers heading for the fort.

"That could have been us a few days ago," he muttered.

At first light the two men had their horses saddled and the gear stowed. The chief stood with his hand on the paint's shoulder. "It is only fair that I warn you," he said to his friend.

"I know," Tom replied. "We are riding into danger. I am ready to die, if necessary, to save my family."

"Yes, to die fighting would be good. But if you are captured alive, Red Wolf will do everything possible to make your last hours painful. He would take pleasure killing your wife first, and maybe your son, before slowly ending your life," the chief warned.

"Then I had best not let them capture me," Tom said, swinging into the saddle. *At least capture me alive,* he thought to himself.

The tall man appreciated that his friend being frank with him. He had no expectations that what lay in front of them would be easy. Thinking back to the fight on the plains, he could see that Red Wolf was a planner. To be successful, they would have to outthink the Crow.

The morning sun was warm on their backs as the two men rode. The tracks of the lookouts were easy to follow. Tom and Two Buffalo kept their horses to a walk, trying to avoid anything that would give cover for an ambush.

Two Buffalo rode wide of the tracks that they were following. Tom noticed that the riders they followed were pushing their horses. That told him that the rest of the party was not too far away.

Less than two miles in front of the two men, the young Crow braves who had occupied the outcrop stopped to give their horses a breather. They were in a heated discussion. Red Wolf had ordered them to watch for the tall white man and the old chief, and then ride to warn the leader.

The larger of the two braves had become disillusioned with Red Wolf, and was trying to convince the slighter one that they should kill Tom and Two Buffalo. They could then ride back to the Crow village with scalps and extra animals.

The smaller brave had to admit that the renegade leader offered them nothing, and had weak medicine. He was also tired of being away from his family and too often riding with an empty belly.

Their pemmican was gone. The braves were forced to eat rodents or other small game, and search for seeds and berries. Red Wolf had only let them kill the pony because of the complaints of having to fight without meat to fill their bellies.

Once in agreement, the two braves planned their ambush. They would work their way back until they located their quarry. They would then take the men down, one at a time.

Unaware that this new danger had arisen in front of them, Tom and Two Buffalo continued following the tracks of the braves. Ralph walked alongside the dun. Tom smiled, thinking that the mule acted more like a dog. Too bad that it didn't range out front like a hunting dog and give warning well before they reached danger.

Tom figured once the lookouts reached Red Wolf, the leader and his braves would ride out and be waiting in a buffalo wallow, a depression, or any washout to ambush them. He looked over at the chief. Two Buffalo rode with a confidence that Tom did not feel.

At midday they stopped and sat on their horses, chewing jerky and sipping from their canteens. "I can feel their eyes on us," the chief said.

Tom had his Hawken across the front of his saddle. Ahead of them, the plain was high above the river and had a series of canyons and washes that ran full when the snow melted. By this time most of them would be dry.

"Should we ride north to the more open plain?" Tom asked.

"If we go north, Red Wolf will make a new plan against us. A battle with him cannot be avoided. A careless move now will mean our death," the chief advised.

The tall man sat, watching the terrain ahead of them. His mouth was dry, making chewing the jerky more difficult. The mule stood grazing a short distance in front of them, showing no concern. That gave him some comfort, believing that the bullet or arrow wouldn't come while they ate.

"We should make some tea," the chief said.

Tom looked at his friend, trying to understand what he had just said. "You think we should have tea . . . now?"

"Yes, over near the short pines on our right," Two Buffalo directed.

Guiding his dun toward the trees, Tom strained his eyes for any movement. The chief rode up and swung off the paint. He loosened the cinch and then started putting a small fire together.

Tom tied the dun to one of the pines, and then dug out their pannikins. He set them onto a rock near the chief and put water into them. "Why the sudden thirst for tea?"

"If I die in the next few minutes, I would like to go to the other side with the memory of one last cup of tea."

"While we drink tea, you think the Crow will come to us?" Tom inquired.

The chief smiled at his friend. "Yes, and we will welcome them."

After sipping a little of his tea, Two Buffalo motioned Tom to be quiet and nodded toward the mule. It was standing, looking north, with its ears forward.

Turning back to his friend, the tall man caught only a glimpse as the chief disappeared behind the pine. Taking a drink of his tea, the tall man looked out at the plain. He adjusted the Hawken in his lap to make it easier to bring into action.

Tom realized that the chief had made the tea in plain sight and had sat out of view. Two Buffalo would work his way around those trying to get close while Tom sat in the open as bait.

Well, he decided, *if you're going to be bait, you might as well be good bait.* He continued to carry on a conversation with what he hoped they would think was the chief. Casually, he set his tea down and loosened his Colt. He reached into his possible bag and brought out another loaded cylinder, tucked behind a piece of hard bread. He noticed the mule continue grazing.

While he sat waiting and chewing the hard bread, he could feel the sweat running down his back. The plain around him was quiet, except for Ralph's grazing. Tom's legs were cramping, and he wanted to get up and move around.

To stand now would just offer a bigger target. He sat and continued acting like he and the chief were talking while watching the mule out of the corner of his eye. Then there was movement to his right!

Dropping his tea, he pulled the Colt. It was Two Buffalo. The chief moved back to his seat and picked up his pannikin.

"The tea has gotten cold," he said, as though disappointed.

"That tends to happen when you leave to take a walk," Tom kidded, relieved to see his friend.

"There are only the two we were following. They watch us from the wash to the left. Their horses are further to the north. I think that is what the mule caught wind of. I think they hope to take our scalps before we find Red Wolf and the others," Two Buffalo explained.

Tom looked at the flat column of rock that the horses were tied near. "How can we avoid them?" Tom asked.

"We can't, Tom. We will ride north around their horses, past the table rock. You will continue riding while I wait for them to come out of the wash. They may try and come at you from behind with a quick hit and run."

"Won't they wonder about you?" the tall man asked.

"We have been riding apart all day. If they have been watching us, they will expect it," the chief told him.

Tom put the pannikins away and tightened the cinch on the dun. Swinging into the saddle, he looked at the table rock. It rose about 30 feet off the plain and was about a half-mile wide.

The two men rode around the pine and cut to the north of the table rock. The chief put some distance between himself and Tom. If they could stop these two Crow, it would cut Red Wolf's strength. It would also prevent them from warning the others, if they hadn't done so already.

Tom came around the other side of the table

rock. He expected to see the braves appear from the crumbled sandstone lying at the base of the rock. If ever he wished for eyes in back of his head, it was now. The sweat running off his forehead burned his eyes.

Blinking to clear them, he looked through the rising heat waves for any movement. The mule was lagging behind, offering him little visual warning. The chief had disappeared while behind the rock.

"You're damn bait again," Tom muttered. He had to admit that if they had to draw them out then he couldn't have a better partner backing him up than the chief.

Less than two minutes after riding past the table rock, Tom heard running horses, followed by the blood-curdling cries of the braves. The mule brayed and ran kicking ahead of the dun.

As he turned the dun to bring the Hawken to bear, there was the crack of the long rifle. Tom watched as the lead brave was knocked off his horse. Raising the Hawken, he fired at the other charging Crow.

The movement of the frightened dun caused his shot to go wide. The brave was pulling back an arrow in his bow. Tom threw his leg over the dun's head and dropped to the ground behind the horse.

He heard the arrow hit something. Drawing the Colt, he stepped out from behind the nervous dun and fired two rapid shots at the charging brave. One of his shots clipped the arm holding the bow, which came loose.

The brave rode past, hanging low behind the animal, offering his leg as the only target. Tom fired twice into the horse, causing it to spill the rider. The Crow tumbled away from the falling horse and came up holding a tomahawk.

Staring into the fear-filled eyes, Tom fired point-blank into the brave. The young Crow stumbled back and sat hard, before falling over sideways. Tom walked over to the fallen brave, keeping the Colt on him. The horse he had shot lay kicking as the life ebbed from it.

Tom heard a horse coming from behind. He glanced back and saw the chief riding towards him. His dun had run a short distance after he'd gotten off. An arrow stuck out of the side of the saddle. Ralph was a quarter-mile ahead of them, looking back.

"You did well," Two Buffalo said as he got off the paint.

"I don't know. I shot too fast with the Hawken, and then just kept shooting at everything that moved," Tom gasped, trying to catch his breath.

"Are you going to keep holding your empty gun on the dead brave?" the chief asked.

A chill ran through, Tom. His Colt was empty. He had loaded only five chambers, leaving the one under the hammer empty. If any had misfired, or had he only wounded the Crow, this could have ended much differently.

Seeing the surprise on Tom's face, Two Buffalo added, "It takes real courage to ride in the open, knowing you will be attacked. You kept your head, and stopped this one from fleeing to join Red Wolf."

While he appreciated the words of praise from the chief, he stood there trying his best to calm his pounding heart.

Looking around, they saw that the other brave's pony was standing three-legged near the table rock. The chief rode up and pulled the saddle pad and hackamore off it.

When he rejoined Tom he said, "I think it bruised a foot during the attack. I gave it freedom to wander and get well."

They left the young braves where they'd fallen, to be picked at and torn apart by the birds and animals of the plain. They rode on to face the next challenge. They were sure that Red Wolf was less than a day's ride from them.

Tom and Two Buffalo passed a stream flowing into the North Platte River just before nightfall. They let the animals drink their fill and then refilled their canteens. They rode an hour after dark and then made a cold, dry camp.

Tom lay under his blankets and thought about the day's events. He was smart enough to know that, along with Two Buffalo's skill, they'd had luck on their side. The arrow that had hit his saddle could have just as easily struck his leg.

He wondered how the chief knew that they were being watched. Had he caught some movement, or noticed the lack of it, or was it simply the sense that eyes were on him? He had noticed Two Buffalo leave their camp to watch and listen after Tom had crawled into his blankets. Was it good that he depended so much on his friend?

Unable to sleep, Tom finally got up and sat in the dark, looking out on the plain. Wolves howled across the vast expanse. Owls hooted and crickets chirped. The air was cool so he draped a blanket over his shoulders.

* * *

Unaware of where her husband might be, Eva lay in the dark, trying to plan her next move. Her first problem would be knowing when to run. If she tried to escape too soon, it would give Red Wolf time to find and recapture her.

Eva spoke softly to Lona. "We need to find a way to warn Tom before they can ambush him."

"You should know that Red Wolf plans to make you his woman," Lona confided. "The brave that has chosen me told me. Even if you were to lose your husband, you will have a strong warrior to take his place."

Inwardly, Eva gasped at the thought. "You must understand that I do not want Red Wolf, and I love my husband," she said, speaking evenly.

It was hard to understand the thinking of the young woman with her. Just a few days ago, her Cheyenne husband had been murdered by these men. Now she spoke as though she was willing to accept one of them and share his blankets.

Closing her eyes, she tried to remember the mouth of the canyon. Was there another way to get up to the top of the walls? Hearing the soft breathing of her fellow captive, Eva decided that Lona was trying to accept that they might be with the Crow for a long time.

The following day, Eva started to venture further from the ledge. She helped with the cooking at the fire. There was a pool of water closer to the mouth of the canyon. She took a wooden bucket and went to fill it.

Red Wolf stopped her. Eva told him that she needed to clean the baby. For a moment it appeared that he was going to send her back to the ledge, but on second thought he walked with her to get the water.

Taking her time, Eva washed her hands and face before filling the bucket. All the time she was memorizing the layout of the canyon. Becoming impatient, the Crow leader pushed the bucket toward her with his foot.

Not wanting to make him angry, she filled the bucket and hurried back to the ledge. Taking her time washing the baby, she thought over what she had seen. The most cover was on the west side of the canyon. She would then have to cross the mouth and climb the east side, which was littered with stunted and downed trees. There were also boulders.

Most nights there had been only one brave guarding them. He watched the ledge where they slept for any movement. The first night, Eva had gotten up to relieve herself. Before she had taken a couple steps from the ledge, a brave had appeared in front of her.

While eating a thin soup the next day, Lona informed her, "The young braves that were watching for riders are late. One was supposed to come and get food for them. No one came."

Eva knew that it was her signal to go. The Crow braves who had left the group before getting to the canyon may have met with Tom. Maybe they'd killed him. It made little difference about going. She could not stay with Red Wolf.

Eva avoided the Crow leader and she took care of the baby and a few other chores around the camp. Several times she noticed Red Wolf staring at her, and the thought of his hands on her made her skin crawl.

That evening, the Crow sat near the canyon mouth, speaking in low voices. When they broke up, one of the men climbed the eastern rim while the others began to make ready to leave the next morning.

There was a small amount of food that Eva had sneaked when helping the braves make meals. It was not much, but by eating sparingly it could last a couple of days. She put Isaac into the cradleboard and waited.

Darkness would fill the canyon and blanket the plain well before the moon would rise. While not a full moon, it would still provide enough light to be spotted moving. The braves in the camp went to their blankets at sundown. She could hear snoring coming from near the fire.

Eva's plan was to move deeper into the canyon before crossing to the other side. Picking up the baby, she moved to the far edge of the ledge. Slipping her hand into the cradleboard, she removed the hidden knife. Her heart pounded in her chest and she prepared to step out.

"Take me with you," a soft whisper reached her ears.

Freezing in mid-step, Eva closed her eyes. She knew that if caught in the escape, the Crow would more than likely kill her or make her wish she was dead. It would be wrong to put Lona and her unborn child in danger. She softly replied, "I will find Tom and come back for you."

Lona rose and stepped close to her. "The brave that has been showing attention to me is on watch tonight. I can help you get by him," she pleaded.

Before Eva had a chance to reply, the young girl moved by her, away from the ledge. The watchful Crow stopped her. They talked briefly and the girl stifled a giggle. They moved away into the darkness.

The sound of a muffled cry was heard, and a

moment later Lona returned with a knife dripping blood. The decision was made. The Cheyenne woman could no longer stay. Without hesitation, the two women went to the other side of the canyon and worked their way along the wall.

As Eva walked she held her breath, hoping that the baby wouldn't fuss. She counted two sleeping braves near the fire. Someone, maybe Red Wolf, would be on the rim watching the plain. In a matter of minutes they reached the mouth of the canyon.

They walked quickly across the open space, expecting to be discovered at any moment. Once in the safety of the east side, they climbed toward the top. If they were spotted by the man on the rim, her plan would be doomed. The thing that would be working for them was that the man would be watching the plain, not the canyon.

The slope was not difficult, and scrub trees hid them from view. Eva thought about the girl following her. Lona had been willing to let the brave think he could make advances toward her to gain his trust. It was evident that while the brave guarding them was reaching for warmth and comfort, Lona had reached for his knife and finished him.

Once at the top of the canyon wall, the desert plain spread out in front of them. While the terrain ahead of them would offer some cover, they would often be exposed. Eva's eyes searched for anyone on the rim.

Satisfied that there was no one nearby, Eva walked bravely onto the plain, with Lona, close behind. At any time, she expected to be grabbed from behind, or struck down by an arrow from Red Wolf or his braves.

They could make several miles before the light of morning would force them to hide. Eva and Lona were walking without moccasins, and the rough, wild, high desert grasses cut at their feet as they made their way.

* * *

Tom sat watching the plain. He had awakened several hours ago and was unable to get back to sleep. Somewhere within a day's ride were his wife and baby. A slow and painstaking search the day before had not revealed any tracks.

When he'd gotten up he'd noticed that the chief's blankets were empty. He didn't know when his friend actually slept. Each night, Two Buffalo would leave. Sometime during the night he would return and be back in camp when the tall man awoke. Maybe it was to watch and listen, or to be closer to nature and the earth. Maybe he just couldn't sleep.

When the sun lightened the eastern sky, Tom gathered some twigs to start a small fire to make coffee. He glanced over and saw that the chief had returned. He lay still, with his back to the fire.

Tom squatted near the fire, roasting coffee beans in the blackened frying pan. He had always believed that the best part of coffee was the smell of getting the beans ready. If just one bean burned, it would ruin the pot.

Crushing the prepared beans with the butt of the Colt, he dumped them into the steaming water.

"Fry up some of the side meat we got at Louie's," Two Buffalo said. "I feel like a hot breakfast."

"Did you want me to serve it in your bed?" Tom asked, kidding his friend.

Sitting up, the chief sat with his legs folded. "There is movement out on the plain."

Tom jerked his head around, looking west of the camp, searching the rugged plain. Slowly, he started slicing the fatty meat into the frying pan as he continued to watch. "There's nothing moving now," he said with a lack of conviction.

A jumble of boulders and a sheer cliff to their backs protected them from the east. If danger came, it would be from the west.

"Last night, something was disturbing life on the desert," Two Buffalo informed Tom.

"Maybe we shouldn't be eating," the tall man said. "Red Wolf and his braves could be crawling toward us right now."

"The Crow wouldn't move at night," the chief assured him. "I do believe we will see Red Wolf or his braves today, so I thought we should do that after a good meal."

"Yes, I know," Tom muttered. "If we go to the other side, it will be with the taste of side meat in our mouths."

The coffee was good and the side meat crisp. They broke up some hard bread into the frying pan to soak up the grease. Tom kept his eyes on the grass-covered plain west of them.

He wished that there was someplace higher, so that he could see further on the plain. The cliff behind them would be difficult to climb, and offered no cover. It would allow them to be spotted from some miles away.

While moving on the desert plain was

dangerous, sitting in one spot worried Tom more. He was anxious to get started, but his friend sat, slowly enjoying his meal.

"The coffee you made is very good. The smell of the beans roasting awoke me this morning," Two Buffalo said with a satisfied look on his face.

The tall man vigorously rubbed the pan with sand to clean it. He attempted to get it into his saddle bag, frustrated with the slow start. "I am glad to see you liked the coffee. The sun has been up most of an hour. We best move before Red Wolf rides right in here."

"Do you have any extra coffee?" a voice came from beyond the camp.

Tom wheeled around, dropping the pan, and drew his Colt. The voice . . . the voice was a woman's! Could it be Eva?

"Come in, but keep your hands in sight," Tom replied, fighting to keep his voice even. Could this be a Crow trick to get their guard down? Would the next few seconds rain bullets and arrows? Tom stood, his eyes straining, for a glimpse of the speaker.

Out of a shallow wash she emerged. It was Tom's wife, with their son. Without hesitation, he ran to meet her, wrapping his arms around his family. Movement beyond her made him look. Lona walked towards the camp.

He noticed that the Colt was still in his hand. Tom dropped it into his holster and took the baby from Eva. She limped into camp ahead of him. Looking down, he saw that she left blood behind with each step.

Lona walked straight to Two Buffalo, put her arms around the Cheyenne chief, and began to cry.

Racking sobs shook her body as she let the pain of her loss come out.

Tom set the cradleboard with little Isaac down against a pine stump. He turned to help Eva.

Grabbing his arms, she looked up at her husband, "You . . . we can't stay here. Red Wolf plans to kill you. That's why he took us. He will follow our trail to you," she said, tears streaming down her cheeks. "We have to run, now!"

"You are safe, Eva," Tom said softly, holding her close. "Ralph will let us know if someone comes, and if they do, we are ready for them."

He realized that the morning breeze was blowing from the wrong direction for the mule to catch the scent of anyone coming from the west at any distance, but his natural instinct was to make her feel like she was protected.

He sat her next to the fire and added wood to the dying coals. Retrieving the frying pan from the ground, he poured water from the canteen and set it onto the fire to heat.

Two Buffalo helped Lona to the fire and sat her next to Eva. There were embedded thorns and multiple cuts on their feet from walking without moccasins through the night.

"How did you find us?" Tom asked.

"By the smell of your coffee," she said, her worried expression finally breaking into a half-smile.

"We walked most of the night, trying to put distance between us and Red Wolf," Eva explained. "We smelled the coffee and meat and headed towards it. Red Wolf had neither, so we knew it had to be a white man, and hoped it was you."

Tom looked up at the chief. "You knew they

were out there. That's why you wanted a hot breakfast."

Two Buffalo smiled at his friend. "I knew something was out there. I hoped it was them. I figured the smell of your cooking would guide them in."

Tom turned to get a spare shirt for bandages when the mule brayed loudly. An arrow passed within inches of the tall man and shattered on a boulder beyond the fire pit. Two Buffalo leaped toward the long rifle lying near his bedroll.

Tom drew the Colt and saw a brave pulling back a second arrow. Leveling the revolver, Tom fired twice at the Crow. The brave jerked as the bullets struck him and the arrow flew wild. Two Buffalo was gone, circling behind the wounded Crow.

Moving back to the fire, Tom crouched in front of Eva and the baby to shield his family. His eyes were fixed on the spot where the brave had disappeared. He saw the barrel of the long rifle rise out of the grass. After it came the chief.

Looking over at Lona, Tom saw her lying on her back, with an arrow protruding out of her shoulder. He went to the injured girl. The arrow had hit her just below the collar bone and hadn't gone through.

The chief came back to the camp. Seeing the wounded girl, he got his blanket roll under Lona's head. He began to cut the deerskin dress to expose the wound.

"There was only one brave. You hit him hard, and he was trying to crawl out on the plain to die. I helped him," Two Buffalo said.

"He could have been the one that was on rim," Eva said. "He must have seen us and followed, hoping we would lead him to you."

For the moment, Tom was overwhelmed. They had two women in need of medical attention. The arrow would be fatal if not removed and treated properly. Somewhere out on the plain was Red Wolf, hunting for them and the women.

The sound of water boiling over onto the coals moved him back to action. Cutting the shirt into strips, he attended to Eva's feet while the chief tried to figure out what was best for the girl.

Using a piece of the shirt, he washed the dirt from the cuts on his wife's feet. With his knife, he removed the thorns as best he could. He then bandaged them with strips of the woolen shirt.

Leaving Eva with the baby, he moved to Lona. Two Buffalo had cut the arrow off, leaving three inches exposed. He had packed some crushed leaves on the wound and rigged a bandage. Wanting to do something to help her, Tom began to tend to her feet.

"I could not remove the arrow," the chief told his friend. "I could not pull it out or push it through. She passed out from pain while I was trying to get it out."

"We need to get her to the doctor at the fort," Tom said.

"She is with child," Eva informed the men.

"She is what?" Tom asked, missing what she had said.

"Eva said she is going to have Tahkeome's baby," the chief said.

The tall man looked at the gray face of the injured girl. Taking her to the fort would mean running for three days in front of Red Wolf as he tried to catch and kill them. The trip would probably be too much for her, and most certainly too much for the fragile child within her.

They had only three animals to ride. That in itself would make travel slow. Looking around the camp, he knew that they could not stay and fight. The area offered poor defenses on all sides, except their backs. Eva could handle a weapon, but they had only two rifles and the Colt Paterson. The chief had his bow.

Tom needed information as he tried to determine what the best course of action was. He turned to his wife.

"How many braves does Red Wolf have?" he asked Eva.

"We left the cabin with Red Wolf and five braves. Two of them were left to watch for you. I do not know where they are now. Lona killed the one watching us in the canyon. You and Two Buffalo killed one here. The most he would have is three," she told him.

"We killed the two on watch," Tom added.

Tom looked at the wounded girl, learning that she had killed the Crow brave. She just might survive a trip to the fort.

All of a sudden, it became clear to the tall man that there was only one solution. He nodded to Two Buffalo to follow him. Stopping out of earshot of the women, he turned to the chief.

"I want you to take the women and the baby and head for the fort. The mule can pull a travois with Lona while Eva rides it," Tom told his friend.

"If I left you out here alone, you would have two hate-filled Crow after you," Two Buffalo warned.

"That is just it, Two Buffalo. They would be

after me, which would keep them off your trail."

"Then you take the women and your son to safety. I will stay behind and wait for the Crow," the chief countered.

"Red Wolf wants me dead. He wants me to die slow and painfully. He took my wife and child to draw me out here. If I take them to the fort, he will go around you and still come after me," Tom said.

The chief knew that it was Tom whom Red Wolf wanted. He wanted to avenge the defeat received during the buffalo hunt. Evidently, the Crow leader believed that Tom had been the leader of the hunting party.

Two Buffalo had no problem accepting that his friend needed to stay and face Red Wolf. He had watched his friend over the years, and was sure that he would be a formidable foe in a fight.

It was Eva who would be the problem. She would not want him left to fight Red Wolf. She would insist on staying to face the Crow with him. Regardless of what happened to him, he wanted her and the baby far from Red Wolf.

Lona needed to have the arrow removed before infection set in and poisoned her system. At any time, Red Wolf and his last follower could show up. If the dead brave out on the plain could follow the women here, the others couldn't be far behind.

The chief watched Tom as he told Eva the plan. She threw her arms around him and violently shook her head no. Two Buffalo did not know what the tall man finally told her, but it worked.

With tears streaming down her face, she took Isaac out of the cradleboard and put him into Tom's arms. She then went to select suitable poles to make the travois. The sound of blows from a hatchet told them that the trees had been found.

The chief brought the mule in to ready it for the travois. Tom walked over, carrying the baby.

"She said if I wanted to go and get myself killed, she at least wanted me to spend my last minutes with my son," Tom explained.

"Your medicine is strong. You will be with your son again, my friend," Two Buffalo responded.

The tall man looked at the confident, lined face of the Cheyenne chief. For some reason, Two Buffalo saw something in Tom that he himself was not sure of. He had heard of people shooting at shadows when they thought they were in danger.

He remembered a hunter whom he had been with when they'd first gotten off the boats in St. Louis. *Never fire blind,* the hunter had told him. *See your target, and then squeeze the trigger.*

Of course, that was so he wouldn't wound a buffalo and stampede the herd. But the words of his prior mentor stayed with him. Isaac, unaware of his father's serious thoughts, laughed as he pulled at the curly beard.

In less than an hour, Ralph was outfitted with the travois. Two Buffalo spoke quietly with Tom before leaving. "Two things have been in our favor. The Crow often come after an enemy alone for individual glory. Also, Red Wolf has lost control of his braves. The attacks on us have not been ordered by him. He likes to come as a group, hit his prey and then run. He will not face you unless forced to. Watch your back."

With that, the chief swung onto his horse and led the way out of camp. Eva looked back and mouthed the words, "I will see you soon."

Tom sat on the dun, thankful to see his family heading for the safety of the fort. He worried about Lona. She lay awake on the travois, her eyes reflecting the pain each jolt caused.

CHAPTER FIFTEEN

Tom turned the horse to the west. Eva had told him of the canyon that they had been held in. She had estimated that they had walked about 10 miles during the night. She had varied the route, to try and cover their trail. It made chills go up his spine, knowing that the enemy was less than a day's ride away.

He urged the dun to move in the direction from which the women had appeared. He spotted the bloody grass from the brave he had shot. Tom followed the blood trail a short distance before he found the dead brave. The Crow lay on his back, with one leg pulled up. Dark holes in the chest and stomach confirmed the accuracy of the tall man's shots. The throat was cut, which showed the chief's effectiveness.

Tom looked across the rolling, broken plain. Filled with swales, water cuts, and buffalo wallows, it would give those hunting him places to hide. He wished that he had the ability to disappear the way Two Buffalo could.

The afternoon sun was bright in the spring sky,

creating sharp shadows across the landscape. Tom thought about the table top that they had passed on the way out. It would give him the high ground to watch for Red Wolf.

He made a loop around the camp where Eva had found him. He made sure that the dun's tracks couldn't be missed so that the Crow would follow him, giving the others time to get away. Tom's nerves were on edge as he rode, expecting death to come from all directions.

It was dark by the time he arrived at the base. Tom had passed the ravaged body of the second brave they had killed. Wolves had torn the corpse apart, leaving scattered bones as the only marker.

Dismounting from the dun, he sat on a pile of rubble with the Hawken across his lap. Tom chewed on jerky and drank water while waiting for the moon to come up. Once the area was bathed in moonlight, he hoped to find a way to the top.

The darkness offered some security from attack. He could blend into the shadows, leaving those looking for him without a target. All afternoon and evening he had the uncomfortable feeling that the enemy was close.

Tom froze in the dark when something ran by, panting. It was probably one of the wolves looking for another meal. He gripped the rifle a little tighter. His dun pranced restlessly, catching wind of whatever went by.

Anxious to find a way up, he led the dun around to the east side of the table rock and searched for a way to get to the top. After an hour of painstaking searching, he found a wall that he would be able to climb.

He had to find someplace to put the horse. A lone cottonwood grew next to a wash just south of the table rock. Some water remained in a low spot from the recent rain. Tom watered the dun before removing the saddle and picketing it near the tree.

Moving from shadow to shadow, he made his way to the table rock. One part of the wall had collapsed when flood water had undercut the base. The pile of broken rock offered a way up.

Struggling for footing in the night, Tom slowly climbed to the top of the table rock. The rough edges of the sandstone tore at his gloved hands. The sound of loose rock falling behind him was unsettling. Anyone within a mile could have heard him in the high desert air.

Despite the coolness of the night, Tom sat on top of the table rock, sweating. He realized that the constant anticipation of coming face-to-face with the Crow was getting to him. He would never stand up to waiting too long for them.

He settled down on the western edge of the table rock and lay on his stomach, looking for any sign of life. Across the river, he caught the flicker of a campfire. Too bad it wasn't that easy to spot the Crow.

He held his breath when he thought that there was movement on the plain below. Tom kept looking, hoping to see what it was. He knew that wolves, coyotes, and large cats moved in the night, looking for something weaker to prey on.

At some point, he dozed. He awoke to the sound of a hawk screeching as it glided over the high desert floor, looking for an early meal. The sun was coming up behind him. Sliding on his stomach, Tom moved away from the edge. He splashed water from his canteen onto his face.

He closed his eyes and listened to the morning sounds. Birds welcomed the new day with songs and hope. He felt some of the tension from the night before leave his body. Tom crawled back to the edge. The sun felt warm on his back.

After three hours, his patience was rewarded. He caught sight of a rider moving along a depression to the west. It was the same route that he had ridden to reach the table rock. It was too far to tell if it was Red Wolf or not. What Tom *was* sure of was that it was one of the Crow hunting for him.

If he continued to follow the dun's tracks, the rider would pass a mound of boulders. Tom realized that he could get to the spot ahead of the brave and surprise him. Pushing back from the edge, his cramping muscles protested. He'd had to lay immobile throughout the morning to prevent anyone below from catching his movement.

Climbing down the east side took much longer than the trip up had taken the night before. Now he could not afford to have the unnatural sound of falling rock, which would alert the rider. The sun was hot against the side of the table rock and sweat ran into Tom's eyes.

Once back on the plain, he ran crouching to the cottonwood. The dun stood with its head up, looking in his direction. If the horse made any noise, it would give his location away. Tom stopped and spoke softly to the animal. It shook its head once it recognized the tall man.

Tom reached the horse and placed his hand over its nose to prevent a snort or whinny. Pulling the picket rope, he led the horse to the pool of water.

While the horse drank, the tall man splashed his face and neck. The water washed the sweat from his eyes.

"I must see the target . . . damn burning eyes."

It took a short time to saddle the dun and ride to the boulders. Tom believed that his quarry was still in the depression and would be unable to see him. He had ridden within a stone's throw of these boulders when coming to the table rock.

Dismounting, he hid his horse on the far side of the mound. Returning to a vantage point to intercept the Crow, Tom settled down to wait. The sun reflecting off the boulders made his position stifling. He held his breath, listening for any sound from the oncoming rider.

He removed the loop from his Colt, to make it ready if needed. Tom held the two trigger Hawken with the rear trigger pulled, which set the front trigger. Tom knelt on one knee, watching, and sweat dripping under his buckskin shirt. A pebble fell from above, landing next to his foot.

He looked up just in time to see the Crow brave leap at him, brandishing a knife in his outstretched hand. Unable to avoid the attacker, Tom swung the rifle in an attempt to deflect the brave's rush.

The barrel of the Hawken struck the knife-wielding arm, causing the blade to narrowly miss its target. The full weight of the brave impacted the tall man, knocking the rifle from his hands and sending both sliding down the bank of a narrow wash, dirt cascading down around them.

Tom was lying on his back as the brave began to get up. The tall man kicked the Crow with his foot to gain the seconds that he needed to get up and draw the Colt. His holster was empty!

The brave wheeled around, coming to his feet with the knife in his hand. Tom saw the Hawken just up the bank, sticking out of the dirt. He scrambled up the slope, just ahead of the charging brave.

Grabbing the Hawken, he spun with one hand on the barrel and the other on the trigger. Tom thrust it at the Crow as he fired. The end of the barrel contacted the brave just under the ribcage. A deafening blast ripped the Hawken from his hands as the brave collapsed on top of him.

Tom saw the gaping hole in the brave's chest. Blood sprayed from the punctured arteries as the man's heart beat its last. Tom pushed himself clear of the Crow. He reached out to catch himself and his left arm failed him. Landing on his stomach, he rolled over into the sitting position.

His arm was covered with blood. At first he thought that it had come from the brave, but now he realized that it was his own. The Hawken lay with its soft iron barrel peeled back. It must have been plugged.

Tom tried to work the fingers of his left hand, but they would not move. The arm and hand were numb. Blood was dripping from a series of cuts on the forearm.

He was in trouble. The brave who had jumped him could not have been the one he'd spotted from the table rock. That meant that the other one had to be Red Wolf. He looked around for the Colt Paterson. It lay at the bottom of the wash.

His head was spinning as he staggered to his feet. Tom stumbled down the bank and picked up the Colt, shaking it to clear any dirt from the barrel. The only hope was to put distance between Red Wolf and himself until he was able to look over his injured arm. Nearly falling several times as he made his way to the horse, Tom expected to hear the cry of the Crow leader at any time.

The dun sidestepped at the smell of blood. Tom grabbed the reins and jerked the horse's head around. "Damn it, horse, if ever there was a time not to be skittish, now is it."

Grabbing the saddle horn with his right hand, he thrust his boot into the stirrup and swung onto the horse. Tom spurred the animal toward the river. As he rode, he left spatters of blood on the plain grass from cuts on his useless arm.

Arriving at the riverbank, he wound his way along the narrow animal trails that weaved through the aspen trees. He spotted an old tree that had been uprooted. It offered him protection from the front, with the river protecting his back.

He dismounted and pulled the saddle bags off with his right hand. He left the dun to wander nearby. His left arm and hand had begun to tingle during the ride, and were now aching. The cuts on his arm were not as bad as he had feared.

The exploding gun barrel must have shocked a nerve, leaving the arm temporarily numb. Tom cleaned the cuts and found metal in two of them. Gritting his teeth, he used his knife to remove them. Then, taking the remaining strips from the shirt used to bandage the women's feet, he fashioned a bandage on his arm.

He sat behind the windfall and watched for any movement that would alert him to danger. Earlier, he realized that he had focused on the rider he had spotted from the table rock. He had failed to make sure that the boulders were clear of danger.

When the dun began to graze closer to the downed tree, Tom caught the reins and tied it behind a growth of tag alders. His tracks from the boulders would be easy to follow. He sat in the rotting leaves and twigs, wondering why the Crow leader hadn't found him.

He looked around his makeshift defense. Right now, Red Wolf could be stealthily moving toward him. Believing that the Crow leader wanted Tom to die slowly, he did not fear a distant gun shot or an arrow.

Red Wolf would appear out of nowhere, the same way that Two Buffalo could. Tom could only hope that during the brief struggle that he would be killed, robbing the Crow leader of the opportunity to kill him slowly.

Tom's arm continued to throb. Having the feeling back in the limb was almost unbearable. The pain was making it difficult to watch for his enemy. How long he would be able to continue staying alert, he couldn't be sure.

In the past, Tom had seen Two Buffalo scrape the inner bark of the aspen and heat it in water. The drink would help reduce pain. The constant ache in his arm finally forced him to light a small fire to heat water.

Depending on the dun to provide some type of warning if Red Wolf got close, he brought out the pannikin and filled it from the river. Setting it next to the fire, he cut some strips of bark from a nearby tree and scraped some of the lining into the water.

Tom kept an eye on the plain while he fixed the drink. The dun remained quiet, nibbling on the tender leaves of the smaller aspens.

The brew of aspen bark was bitter, and difficult to swallow. Finishing the drink, he took advantage of the fire and heated a second cup. He removed the bandage and grimaced at the sight of ugly bruises and cut flesh.

Dipping a piece of cloth into the hot water, he began to clean the arm. While still painful, the ache seemed to be lessening. He covered the cuts with the bark poultice before putting the bandage back on.

The sun was going down. Tom had loosened the cinch on the dun's saddle, but he kept it on in case of a quick departure. He began to second guess if the rider he had seen was Red Wolf or not.

Tom slept little that night. The constant ache could only be decreased by holding the arm up toward the sky. The strength of the grip remained weak. Well before daylight, he gave up sleep and decided to move away from the river.

By the time the sun came up, he was near the table rock. He had ridden wide of his prior route to the river. Tom planned to look for any evidence of the rider that he had seen. He rode slowly toward the cluster of boulders.

The dun's tracks were clear on the sandy ground. He dismounted and led the horse to the site of the attack. The brave whom he had shot was gone!

The sign around the area told a clear story. A rider had come from the direction of the depression. The body of the brave had been loaded onto the horse and the rider had led the animal toward the west.

He'd led the horse right over the dun's trail. The hoof marks were clear, yet the man leading the horse with the dead brave did not hesitate when passing them.

Was he trying to lead Tom into a trap? Sitting on the dun, he looked west, where the man had gone. Red Wolf had been killing and robbing for some time. Eva had told Tom about the canyon where the renegade Crow kept a store of supplies.

The tall man wondered if the trail would lead to the canyon. By all appearances, that was exactly where the man he was following was going. Tom rode slowly, staying wide of anything that would give the Crow an ambush site.

The man's trail did not deviate from the westward trek. The disturbed grass and dirt on the high desert continued to display evidence of his quarry throughout the day.

The ground began to become more broken from spring flooding and ancient rivers. The North Platte River wound in a green valley below the sparse growth of the high ground on which Tom was traveling

He stopped for the evening and made a camp without a cook fire. He sat wrapped in his blankets and chewed hard bread and jerky. Water from his canteen washed the tough meal down.

Crickets filled the night air with sound. Wolves called to each other as they hunted. A mockingbird competed with an owl to rule the night. The beauty of the desert night was lost on Tom.

Somewhere nearby was Red Wolf, who was intent on killing him. Tom knew that when they met, it would be kill or be killed. He sat against a scrub pine in the chill of the night and held his Colt Paterson in his lap. It seemed like the blankets didn't offer any warmth.

Exhausted from the lack of sleep, even the ache of his arm didn't keep him awake. He dreamed that he was chasing some unseen thing. It kept circling around and getting behind him. He would hear a shot and feel something hit his back, but it didn't seem to hurt or stop him. Tom would turn and pursue the thing again. He awoke shortly before first light, wondering if the dream meant anything.

Even though the morning air was cool, Tom was covered with sweat. He removed the bandage from the arm and let the morning air at the wounds. He had cut the sleeve off the buckskin shirt to stop it from rubbing against the scabbed cuts.

Rolling up the blankets, he set them with his gear. He went to get the dun and brought it closer. By the time he had saddled the horse and secured his gear, Tom was winded. He leaned against the horse to catch his breath.

He knew that his time and strength were limited. Tom was thankful that the chief, Lona, and his family had been given time to make for the fort. He tried to think of how close they might be, and couldn't be sure. The past few days ran together in his thoughts.

With the sun just breaking the horizon behind him, Tom continued west. In less than a mile, he came to a canyon. It had to be the one that the women had been brought to. A well-worn path led down to the mouth.

To his right were the rocks and scrub growth that had given Eva the cover to make her escape. Tom rode to the floor of the canyon. He continued riding in the middle of the opening. From inside the canyon he could hear shouting, or chanting.

Tom stopped the dun when the Crow leader came into sight. Red Wolf stood near a blazing fire deeper into the canyon. He was singing a medicine song, holding a stick with a fiery brand and touching the glowing tip to his chest.

On a makeshift pole and hide alter, lay the body of the brave killed yesterday. Near the fire were rifles taken during the raids. Red Wolf was looking toward the sky, shouting and ranting in Crow. His eyes were wild and his face was twisted in rage.

Tom did not speak or understand the Crow language. He sat on the horse staring at the sight. "The son-of-a-bitch has gone crazy," he said in wonder.

Suddenly, Red Wolf stopped. He had noticed Tom. The leader's eyes grew round and his lips pulled back from his clenched teeth. Throwing the stick into his fire, he pointed at the tall man and shouted, "I will kill you, Tom Franklin! Then I will watch while the buzzards pick at your eyes!"

Swinging down from the dun, Tom pulled the Colt and started walking toward the Crow. While he had no idea what Red Wolf was saying, he found himself yelling at the man, "You're a yellow dog! Like a coward, you hide in this canyon while you're brave men come out and fight for you!"

Tom's Colt was out of range for a handgun. The rifles near Red Wolf were in effective range. He regretted not riding the horse closer. He walked briskly to close the distance.

Red Wolf was ranting out of control. Tom was surprised that the Crow was hurling insults rather than picking up a weapon. "When you are dead, I will take your woman and kill your son. She will know that you were weak, and come with me!" Red Wolf kicked the burning wood and sent sparks into the air.

Tom walked rapidly and snarled, "You crazy bastard! Let's finish this!"

While neither knew what the other was saying, the verbal confrontation was sending the needed adrenaline into Tom's system that would provide him with the strength required for the fight.

Red Wolf continued to scream, "After I saw her on the plain, the great spirit told me that she would be mine. Together we would lead all the tribes and push the white man out of our lands."

The Crow appeared to have lost control. He stomped his feet and shook his fists at Tom. Meanwhile, the distance between the two men had closed. Red Wolf abruptly seemed to realize this and picked up a long rifle, aiming it at Tom.

Smoke and fire burst from the muzzle. The ball burned across the top of the tall man's shoulder, spinning Tom and causing him to fall.

From the ground, Tom shouted, "You attack women and children because you are weak. You kill from hiding, because you are afraid to face your enemy!"

He leaped back to his feet and continued toward Red Wolf.

The Crow leader grabbed the Mackinaw gun and threw it in Tom's direction. "That is my brother that you killed! For his death I will make you stay alive to suffer unbearable pain! While you beg, I will take your scalp as a prize for your woman."

Tom leveled the Colt Paterson and squeezed the trigger. The gun misfired. Twice more he pulled the trigger without results. He then roared and ran at the Crow leader raising the revolver to use as a club.

Red Wolf glared at the tall man with a look of pure hate and drew his knife. Tom knew that time had run out.

With anger and hate driving the two men, they came together, slamming into each other, the impact echoing in the canyon. They tumbled to the ground, rolling several times, attempting to gain control and advantage on the other.

Tom gripped the arm wielding the knife, preventing the blade from being plunged into him. His attempt to brain Red Wolf with the barrel of the Colt had resulted in an ineffectual glancing blow.

Dust from the canyon floor rose as a cloud obscuring the struggle. Red Wolf managed to get on top of Tom and strained to bring the blade across his enemy's face. Gathering all his strength, the tall man brought his feet under the thighs of the renegade and shoved, sending the Crow backwards over the dead brave, collapsing the poles.

The two men regained their feet and slowly circled. Tom had lost the Colt and now had his knife out. The front of his buckskin shirt hung open in the front, the result of a swipe from Red Wolf's blade.

All of a sudden, the Crow leaped forward. Tom, holding his knife low, brought it up to meet the renegade while turning to avoid Red Wolf's slash. He felt the impact of his blade sinking into the belly of the Crow.

The momentum of the attack sent both men back to the ground. Tom thrust and twisted the knife, feeling his enemy's blood flowing over his hand and down his arm. Red Wolf attempted to raise himself away from the blade. His strength gone, he wilted. The tall man pushed the dying Crow off him.

Slowly, Tom got to his feet, pulling his knife from the man's stomach. He looked down at the bleeding renegade leader. Red Wolf tried to speak as he gasped for breath. His eyes went from Tom to the sky above. He began to sing his death song, which turned into a rasping cough. Then he was gone.

The tall man stood over the lifeless body. The emotions flooding over him were overwhelming. While he knew that the danger of this man was over, Tom still raged.

He held the bloody knife, wishing that he could punish the dead leader more. As the rage subsided, Tom sank to his knees, his shaking legs unable to support him.

CHAPTER SIXTEEN

Tom sat next to the lifeless body of Red Wolf. His mind drifted back to the first fight on the buffalo hunt. If he had only had another bullet in his Colt when he'd first seen the scarred face of this man, none of this would have happened.

He wondered what Red Wolf had shouted at him. One thing that Tom was sure of was that it had been personal and that the Crow leader's hatred had been aimed at him.

Before leaving the canyon, Tom found that a small piece of stone had lodged in the revolver, preventing it from firing. After cleaning it, he reloaded the Colt. He then packed the items that he recognized from the cabin, and the rifles near the fire, on two of the Crow's horses. The Mackinaw gun was included in the packs.

He left Red Wolf and the other brave where they lay. The wild plains animals would take care of them. Tom pulled the dun up for a few minutes at the mouth of the canyon. He searched the tops of the walls behind him. There was always the chance that there were other followers of Red Wolf.

A jolt went through him as he realized the danger that he had just faced. He wondered how many brushes with death a person could face before it caught up. Tom shrugged the shoulder that had been burned by Red Wolf's first shot. A few inches over and it would have been a neck shot.

One of the horses that he had packed was a good-looking sorrel, and was shod. No doubt it had been recently stolen by the renegades. The other was an underfed mustang. He urged the dun on and followed the trail towards the river.

After arriving at the north bank, he saw a raft loaded with goods making its way toward the fort. Two barefoot men pushed it in the slow current with poles. Sitting in the front were two women and three children.

While Tom rode he smiled, thinking about his own family. He wished that the family below was his. With a family there should be something that he could do that would be safer than fighting the winters in the mountains to eke out a living.

One thing that he knew about was farming. He had left Vermont to get away from the boredom and drudgery of pulling a living out of the dirt. He and his brother had headed west to find adventure.

Trapping in the mountains gave a man the thrill of majestic surroundings and the challenge of outwitting the animals he was after. While doing so, he trespassed on lands long claimed by the mountain tribes.

Most mountain men found a way to get along with the Blackfoot, Crow, Flathead, and the others that they might encounter. They would trade goods for furs and often marry women from their tribes.

The mountains were without the laws and structure that was found in the towns to the east. If someone wanted what another had and was stronger, or without morals, they could take it.

It was often an eye for an eye, with a good measure extra when the injured party rode for revenge. All too often, innocent parties like Wally and the Flathead woman got in the way.

It was just by chance that killers got caught. There was no marshal to take up the chase, or a judge passing sentence. A mountain man rode among the peaks, knowing the risks that he was taking. But it was his own life that he was responsible for, not others.

If he took his wife and child into this lawless environment, he would never be able to forgive himself if harm came to them. While the majority of the mountain men lived by a code that would bring no harm to women and children, the isolation that they lived in provided little help if trouble came.

Tom stopped at a creek and watered the horses. He was near the table rock and thought about the Hawken rifle. He turned the dun toward the mound of boulders. It still lay where he had dropped it.

Swinging down, he stretched his stiff muscles. The trampled dirt still showed evidence of the blood that had spilt from the brave. He picked up the destroyed weapon and rubbed his hand over the wooden stock and steel butt plate.

It had been a good long gun and had provided him a living and food in the west. It had been too good to now leave it on the high desert to rust. Putting it onto the pack horse, he swung back onto the dun. Reaching back, he took some jerky from his saddle bag.

He continued along the river toward the fort. It would be two, maybe three days before he would reach it. He hoped that the Cheyenne woman had survived the trip, and that the doc at the fort had been able to fix her up.

Tom continued pondering his future. Would it be buffalo hunting? He doubted that the herds would last too many more years. Across the plains were the bleached bones of the wooly beasts. They were hunted by both plains men and Indians.

Hunting buffalo had its own dangers, but somehow it didn't have the isolation of the mountains. At any given time, the hunters could quit and head for a fort, or trading post. Snow blocking the passes, and the dangers of slippery trails, made leaving the mountains impossible during the winter.

Tom thought of a hunter's life living next to a buffalo hide wagon. The grasslands covered with the rotting carcasses; the smell, the flies, the drudgery. Yes, the drudgery of skinning the wooly beasts. He might as well be farming. At least on a farm there was a hot bath every Wednesday and Saturday night. When buffalo hunting, the stink clung and there was no chance of a bath.

He made camp near the lookout rocks that the two Crow braves had stayed at. Tom looked across the river, and in the distance he saw two riders leading packhorses loaded with their catch of beaver.

Collecting some branches below a cluster of aspen, he built a fire. In the west, the sun was setting, painting the sky with red and orange. Tom broke out his coffee pot and put some water to heat.

He unwrapped a cloth cover from a chunk of salt pork. Slicing several generous pieces into the blackened frying pan, he set it onto the coals. Sitting back, he thought about Louie at the fort.

That would be a good line of work. You spent time with mountain men when they brought in their furs. You enjoyed their stories about the mountains while living a safe and comfortable life next to the protection of a fort.

The problem with that idea was the lack of money to buy into, or start up, a trading post. A second, and even bigger problem, was that he would spend his days looking at the mountains and no longer get into them.

The excitement and longing to ride among the peaks was still strong in Tom's soul. He might as well be back in Vermont if it was just a living that he was after. He wondered why just being with Eva and his child wasn't enough. Was he wrong for wanting more?

Before eating, he checked his Colt and leaned a long rifle that he had chosen from Red Wolf's cache within easy reach. Using his knife, Tom speared slices of the crisp, salty meat and blew on them before devouring the pork. He filled his pannikin with strong coffee and closed his eyes as he sipped the brew.

Out on the plains, the sounds of wolves, coyotes, doves, and crickets filled his ears. This was the life that he had always dreamed of: The freedom of the wide-open spaces and enjoying a meal over a crackling fire.

The pannikin settled on Tom's lap and his head tilted forward as he dozed. He was worn out from the past several days of chasing Red Wolf and worrying that at any time he could be attacked.

"Your coffee is getting cold."

Startled by the voice, Tom grabbed for his long rifle, spilling his pannikin. His hand missed the grab and knocked the weapon over. He turned and looked at the speaker.

The wise eyes of Two Buffalo looked at him from across the dying fire. "Damn, you scared me sneaking up like that," Tom complained.

"If I had been Red Wolf, you would have been dead. It is not healthy for a man to sleep so soundly," the chief advised.

"Well, if you had been Red Wolf you would have had to be a ghost," Tom answered. "His body is rotting in a canyon back a ways."

"And the others?"

"All dead too, the best I can figure," Tom answered. "I am glad you are here. How was the trip to the fort? How is the Cheyenne girl?"

Two Buffalo removed the cup hanging from his waistband and filled it with the stale coffee. After taking a taste, he replied, "The fort doctor took the arrow out. It was caught on a bone. He says she has a good chance of getting well."

"Eva and Isaac?"

"Eva wanted to come back with me. Louie's sister offered to watch the boy. I convinced her to stay at the fort and help with Lona. I promised her that I would bring you back unhurt."

Tom poked a couple more sticks of wood into the fire. "We can get an early start. She has had to worry too long already."

"The army is offering a reward for the capture of Red Wolf. You should be able to get that for killing him," Two Buffalo said. He took another sip of the coffee and made a wry face. He then tossed out the remainder.

Tom stood and looked around. "Where is your horse? I'll water it before we turn in."

"You take care of the dun. I'll be back after taking a look around the area," the chief said.

As the tall man turned, the fire lit his left side. Two Buffalo saw the bandage and bruising. "Your arm is hurt. Was it Red Wolf?"

"No, the barrel of the Hawken got plugged with mud and I fired it. When the barrel split it damn near felt like it took the arm off," Tom said. "It weren't as bad as it felt, though. It should be alright."

The dun whinnied as Tom approached to pull up the picket stake and lead it to water. He could hear the paint walking away from the camp. In the morning he would awaken and the chief would be back in camp.

The sun was up when Tom awoke. He couldn't believe that he had slept in. Having his friend back with him had decreased his worries more than he had realized. He looked over and Two Buffalo was at the fire, making coffee.

"I'm sorry I slept so late," Tom apologized.

"You needed it," Two Buffalo said, pouring steaming coffee into their pannikins.

Accepting the hot coffee, Tom said, "I want you to know that I was damn happy to see your wrinkled face."

The chief sliced side meat into the blackened frying pan. As it started to snap and sizzle, he pushed it around with the point of his knife. Once the meat was crisp, he put it on two tin plates and added some biscuits from his saddlebags.

Accepting the plate of food, Tom shoved a

whole slice of the side meat into his mouth. While it burnt his tongue, it was mighty tasty. The biscuits were a bit dry, so he dunked them into his coffee.

By mid-morning they had a couple miles behind them. Tom noticed that the chief had an extra leather bag hanging from his saddle. Two Buffalo had expected a long trip and had brought extra supplies, Tom guessed. He was thankful that they were not necessary.

CHAPTER SEVENTEEN

Two days of steady riding brought them to within sight of the fort. The workers were busy building the new fort. With the stockade removed, Louie's trading post stood in the open. The rest of the buildings that had once made up Fort William seemed to be naked without the walls around them.

Pulling up to the trading post, Tom tied the dun and pack horses to the chewed rail. Two Buffalo pointed toward the small structure used by the fort doctor and turned his paint in that direction.

As Tom stepped onto the worn, wooden porch, he heard a commotion coming from inside. There was the sound of wood splintering, and metal cans or pots falling to the floor.

Tom loosened the Colt as he headed toward the door. He stepped into the dim room. Before his eyes had a chance to adjust to the light, a thrown object hit him and knocked the tall man back out the door.

Sprawling in the muddy street, Tom dodged between the horses, trying to avoid their thrashing legs.

Regaining the porch, he lunged into the low room and ducked to one side.

A large trapper with stained buckskins was wrecking the place and questioning the prices Louie was willing to pay for his furs. There were several things from the shelves scattered across the floor.

Anger surged through the tall man. He strode over, grabbed the smelly trapper, and spun him around. Without a word, Tom hit him across the jaw with a roundhouse punch.

The punch was delivered with all of the built-up anger from the time when he had found Eva gone. The trapper went backward, stumbling. Spinning, he landing face down in the middle of the room.

Louie came around the counter with a short club raised, ready to put the man back down if he tried to get up. "This damn business is getting too rough. The son-of-a-bitch comes in here with rodent-chewed furs, expecting top price. Wait until he has to deal with the American Fur Company. They will send him packing with trash like he brung in."

Shoving a broken stool out of the way, Tom walked up to the counter, trying to force himself to calm down. Louie went back behind the counter and set the club on a shelf.

Looking from Tom to the unconscious trapper, he said, "I am sorry you had to walk in on this." Straightening his shirt and slicking back his hair, he asked, "What can I get for you, Tom?"

"I'm looking for Eva," the tall man said.

"She is over at the doc's, helping with the Cheyenne girl," Louie said. "I was supposed to bring some canned goods to them. If you could take them with you, I would appreciate it." Sighing, he continued,

"As you can see, I have quite a mess to clean up."

"One more thing, Louie," Tom said. "I got a skinny mustang out front with some rifles. Look them over and let me know what they're worth to you."

He picked up the sack of goods that the merchant had prepared for the doc. Tom untied the dun and sorrel, then led them toward the small building that the doctor used. He looked back at the trading post and saw Louie tossing the trapper into the street, next to a pile of scattered furs.

Tom tied the horses next to Two Buffalo's paints. He walked up to the office door and then hesitated, debating whether he should knock or just go in. Before he could decide, the door was flung open and Eva rushed out, throwing her arms around him.

"I was so worried about you," she said, burying her face in his shirt and starting to cry.

"I am okay. Please don't cry, Eva," he pleaded.

Putting his arm around her shoulder, they entered the doctor's office. The familiar smell of lye was strong in the room.

Doc Ward was busy extracting a tooth from a teamster. The sounds of the gruesome metal tool grinding against the tooth, combined with the groans of the man, filled the room. Eva guided the tall man to the back room.

Two Buffalo sat next to Lona, talking in a low voice. He looked up at Tom and Eva as they entered. The hollow-eyed Cheyenne girl gave them a weak smile.

"Eva was very worried about you, Tom. I am glad you are back. Two Buffalo told me that you killed Red Wolf," Lona said, her voice weak from her ordeal.

"I am fine and won't be leaving again soon,"

Tom replied. "I do want to thank you for helping Eva escape."

The four of them continued to talk in hushed tones while they tried to ignore the suffering teamster in the wooden chair. When Tom heard the doc giving instructions on the extraction area of the man's mouth, he excused himself and went into the front office to talk to the doctor.

Doc Ward was standing at a small table and washing the dental tools in a porcelain basin. Glancing back, he said, "I will be right with you, Tom. I got another fellow waiting outside with some broken teeth. I got to clean these for him."

"There is a good chance I met the man earlier," Tom confided, rubbing his knuckles.

"Well, I do appreciate the business you are drumming up for me," the doc kidded.

Suddenly, he stopped talking as he noticed the crude bandages on Tom's left arm. "Let me take a quick look at that arm."

The doctor removed the bandages and looked at the injured limb, shaking his head. "Damn poor job of doctoring. Then again, I have seen worse."

After applying some stuff from a blue bottle, he wrapped it in clean bandages. Tom gritted his teeth, bearing the sting of what the doctor had swabbed on.

As the doc turned to put the blue bottle back, the tall man said, "I want you to know that I will pay for Lona's care."

"Well, your wife has been a great help with the girl and has assisted with many other things in the office. I would say we are even, except for a few medical supplies," Doc Ward answered back.

"For that, I thank you, Doc."

Setting the extractor pliers on the small table next to the wooden chair, the white-haired doctor nodded towards the door. "I best get the next fellow in here."

Tom smiled and said, "And I best get back to the other room. I am not sure he would be happy to see me."

While the doctor was pulling the broken teeth from the trapper, the three promised Lona that they would be back in the morning and left the office. Tom suggested that they go eat at the Buffalo Hide Saloon.

They left the doctor's office and brought their horses to the livery. After instructing the hostler to give the horses extra grain, a good rubdown, the three of them walked down the tree-lined path, looking forward to a hot meal at the saloon.

While they waited for their meal to be served, Tom tasted the mug of beer Louie's sister had brought to the table. The chief drank tea, while Eva chose water. One of the girls who worked for Louie's sister was watching Isaac.

Taking a deep breath, Tom leaned back and said, "I got to thinking about what I should do next. We have the cabin to go back to, but no way to earn money there. We could go buffalo hunting, or I could see if the soldiers need someone to help with hunting for meat."

Tom fell silent as the meal of venison stew was brought to the table. A hot loaf of bread and a bowl of butter were placed in the middle of the table. Louie's sister said, "After you eat that up, I got some minced meat pie for dessert."

The chief picked up a slice of the bread and smeared butter on it. Satisfied with the results, he took a bite and a look of approval was on his face. Swallowing the bread, he looked across the table at Tom.

"Why do you worry about making money? The good earth gives a man most things he needs. The rest you trade for or take from your enemies," Two Buffalo advised.

Eva poked at her stew, deep in thought. Tom noticed that she wasn't eating. "Eva, is something wrong with the meal?"

"No. The meal is very good. I was wondering, what you want to do? I watch you hunting buffalo. It is something you do well, but it doesn't seem to make you happy. If you want to be a mountain man, I will stay behind and wait for you to return. I know you don't want to farm. You left your home in the east because it was not enough." She hesitated a moment before finishing. "I want you to know that I will be with you in whatever you choose to do."

Two Buffalo looked at Eva and seemed pleased with her willingness to defer to her husband.

Tom smiled at his wife. "You are right about hunting buffalo. I would put that right up there with farming."

The chief scraped the last spoonful of stew from his dish. He then placed the bowl to the side. "While I don't understand why it is, but you do seem to get great pleasure out of building things and working with wood."

Louie's sister came to the table and collected the bowls. "I will be right back with your pie. Would everyone like some coffee?"

They all nodded and watched as she came back with three generous slices of pie. After setting them down, she stepped back and said, "It may not be my place to say anything, but I couldn't help but overhear your conversation. If you are looking for something to do, my brother has talked of selling the trading post and spending his time here at the saloon."

Tom ate his pie in silence. It was ironic that she mentioned Louie selling. He had even considered becoming a merchant on the ride back from the canyon. Unfortunately, living and working near the fort would lack the excitement that he wanted in life.

As usual, the chief left to go somewhere in the night, leaving Tom and Eva alone. They arrived at the room that she had been staying in. The baby was already sleeping. The young lady who was watching him left to go back to the saloon.

Tom washed up at the side table. What he needed was a long, hot bath. Eva brought him a towel and helped him off with his shirt. She gasped as she saw the bruises extending above the bandage on the arm.

"Don't worry, Eva," Tom assured her. "The doctor looked at it and put some stuff on it. He said I did a good job fixing it up."

He finished washing and then ran his fingers through his unruly hair and beard. His eyes were on his wife as she walked across the room to their bed.

Eva pulled back the covers, and lowered the lamp wick. She slipped off her dress and lay on the bed, waiting for her husband to finish undressing. It had been months since they had lain together. They had much to make up for.

* * *

The next morning, Tom left the room early to meet with Two Buffalo. He looked back at his wife, bathed in the early morning light, as he closed the door. He knew that there was no way that he could leave her for another winter of trapping.

He walked up the path to meet his friend. Suddenly, Tom was in a sullen mood. He was unaware of the sunshine, soft breeze or the birds singing. He realized that the dream of living the life of a mountain man had died. He had made the decision that love of family had to come first.

The chief was waiting for him near the livery. The paint was saddled and ready to go. Tom waved as he walked up to his friend.

"I thought we were going to talk to the army about Red Wolf," he said, confused as to why Two Buffalo had the horse saddled.

"After we talk to them, I will be taking Lona to her family," the chief explained. "They will take care of her."

Tom noticed that there were bags hanging from the saddle horn. "Bringing the family some extra food?"

Two Buffalo smiled and led the paint toward the army headquarters. The army would eventually be in the new fort, but during construction they occupied some clapboard buildings overlooking the Laramie River.

A sergeant had a detail of men cleaning the grounds around the headquarters. He was a short, barrel-chested man who seemed to enjoy barking orders at the privates. He looked up at the two arrivals and put his hands on his hips.

"Can I help you?" the sergeant asked.

"We are here to claim the reward for killing Red Wolf," Tom answered.

Rubbing his chin, the abrasive sergeant looked them over. "I heard that someone had killed the renegade. You got some proof that it was you? I don't see no body."

"The body is lying in a canyon three day's ride up the Laramie," the tall man said, trying not to let the sergeant's demeanor bother him.

"Well, when you go fetch it, I will present it to the major and get you your money," the sergeant said and then turned to watch his men work.

Tom was tempted to spin the cocky soldier around, when Two Buffalo put his hand out to stop his friend. Walking around the paint, the chief took down a bag. Opening the top of it, he tossed its contents toward the sergeant.

"Here's your proof," Two Buffalo said as the renegade leader's head rolled to the feet of the sergeant.

Shocked at the sight of the head, the barrel-chested soldier cried out and jumped out of the way.

"What the hell?" he demanded.

"That is the head of Red Wolf," the chief snapped. "If you want more, I will get the rest of the rotting carcass and put it on your desk."

"Get that damn thing out of here!" the sergeant ordered.

"Not until we get the reward," Tom said, displaying a cruel smile. "You wanted proof. It is lying right in front of you, scar and all."

The flustered sergeant turned and stomped into the headquarters office. The two men could hear a loud discussion on the inside, followed by silence.

The office door opened and a middle-aged

major with a bushy red moustache stepped out. He looked at the two men and then at the head lying on the ground.

"I want to apologize for my sergeant. He says you claim to have killed Red Wolf."

"It's more than a claim, Major." Pointing to the head, Tom said, "That head with the scar on the cheek was Red Wolf."

Stepping off the porch, the major looked at the head. "Yep, I can see the scar. I believe you have brought the proof you need. Give me a minute and I will send Sergeant Oaks out with some papers to sign, and your money."

When the sergeant came back out, he was all smiles. He had Tom sign a verification document and then handed him $100. "I never did see that Red Wolf before. The major recognized him by the scar."

Thanking him for the money, Tom and Two Buffalo turned to leave. The sergeant called after them, "Ain't you gonna take the stinking head with you?"

Tom replied over his shoulder, "It wouldn't be right if we did. The army paid good money for it."

Walking away, they heard Sergeant Oaks cussing and instructing one of his men to get the damned thing out of the compound and bury it.

Two Buffalo stopped short of the doctor's. "I expected them to want proof. When you told me that Red Wolf was lying in the canyon, I went there in the night. I figured having his head would be enough."

"I thank you for doing that. Half of the reward is yours. Without the head we would be leaving with empty pockets," Tom said.

"You can give my half to Eva and Isaac. As you know, I have little need for white man's money."

224

With a smile on his face, the chief continued to Doc Ward's to pick up Lona.

Tom stopped just off the path and sat on a bench suspended between two oak trees. He looked toward the construction of Fort John. The name did not sound right to him. It had been Fort William when he had first arrived on the plains, and the name suited it.

Lots of the locals had called it Fort Laramie because it was build next to the river. His eyes followed the river west. The morning was clear, and he was able to see the blue outline of the mountains low on the horizon.

A mourning dove called out to its mate. The sound of hammering came from the direction on the new fort. Somewhere, a rusty pump handle complained as someone drew water for breakfast.

He looked around at the various buildings. If he could not go to the mountains and earn a living, he could find work around the fort. They could spend summers at the cabin and build a barn, plant a garden, and maybe even put in a cash crop.

It might not be so bad to raise the family on a farm. They had almost $400 from trapping and the reward to start a life here. As he sat, the warmth of the morning sun and the freshness of the day elevated his mood.

He heard someone coming up the path. Looking over, he saw Eva carrying Isaac. She was singing softly to the baby. Tom was suddenly feeling better about his decision. Remembering how he had felt when leaving the boarding house that morning made him feel ashamed.

After spending the night with his soft, loving

wife, he had let the warm feelings be pushed aside by his own selfish desires to trap and hunt the high country. Removing his hat, Tom ran his fingers through his hair.

"Where are the two of you going on this beautiful morning?" he asked.

"I came to find you," she said, taking a seat next to him.

Handing Isaac to his father, she said, "After you left this morning, I got to thinking about when I was young. I remembered a trip my father had taken our family on. A severe winter had killed off much of the game around our village. He talked of a creek of boulders that he had hunted in his youth."

Tom broke into her story. "I once met a trapper that talked of such a creek near Fort Jackson. I believe he said it flowed into the South Platte River north of the Vasquez River."

"That could be the one that my father took the family to. We traveled south for several days," Eva said. "I remember that when we got there, the hunting was good and we ate well. But even more important, the mountains that the creek ran through were beautiful. We spent the summer there. I believe it was the happiest summer of my life."

"You mean even happier than our last summer?" he kidded her.

"Tom Franklin, hunting buffalo with you last summer was good. But, the plains wasn't quite as nice as the creek of boulders," she said, pretending to pout.

"I imagine they weren't," he said, giving her an affectionate hug. "Eva, I have decided that I am going to find work near the fort. We can continue to build near the cabin in the summers. Maybe we will put in crops to sell. We can even raise some horses or cattle."

Tom stood up, still holding the baby and looked toward the Laramie River. He was surprised that just saying it took a weight off his shoulders. "Dragging my family out on the plains, with all the dangers of hunting buffalo, or leaving you behind for months while I trap in the mountains, is wrong."

Eva joined her husband and they slowly began to walk toward the river. "Your dream had been to be a mountain man. You told me you left your home back east to get away from farming. Now you say that we should become farmers."

"It was just an idea, Eva. Maybe I could get a job helping to build the new fort. There will also be a need for other buildings as more people come west."

They walked in silence under the cottonwood trees lining the river bank. Eva looked at her tall husband beside her. She couldn't see him being happy building other people's homes, with the mountains just out of his reach. She would have to choose her words carefully.

"I know your decision must have been a hard one. We have faced difficult times and danger over the past year. Living around the fort would be safer," she said, stopping, taking little Isaac from Tom. "I must also be willing to give up my dream of going back to the creek of boulders."

"Your dream?" Tom asked, surprised at her revelation.

"Yes," Eva said. "I pictured us living near the creek in the mountains. Maybe we could trade goods for furs."

"You wanted us to open a trading post?" Tom asked.

"Not just a trading post. A trading post run by a mountain man," she said, smiling at the thought.

"Where would we get supplies?" he asked.

"Louie wants to get out of the business. We could buy stock from him. There is money from trapping," she suggested.

"That we have," Tom agreed. "Also, there is the money from the reward."

"Reward?" she asked.

"That's right, the army gave me and the chief $100 for killing the Crow leader," he said.

"Well, that may be more than enough to stock a place," Eva concluded.

A shout from the trail above the river interrupted the conversation. "Well, look at the happy family, enjoying a morning walk."

Looking up, they saw Chess sitting on his buckskin.

"You're looking a hell of a lot better than the last time I saw you," Tom called back.

"I owe it to clean living and staying close to the fort. You should try it," his buckskin-clad friend recommended.

"Thanks for the advice," Tom said, putting his arm around Eva. "But I think our next stop is the creek of boulders, in the mountains south of here."

CHAPTER EIGHTEEN

Filled with excitement at the prospect, the couple headed back for the boarding house. Tom sat on the chair near a small table that held the lantern. Eva sat on the edge of the bed and began to nurse Isaac. On the table, Tom had a piece of packaging paper and a short pencil. He began by sketching a map of what he knew of the area south of Fort John.

"I wish I had spent more time talking to the fellow that had been to Fort Jackson" Tom said. "He mentioned that there were other forts, or trading posts on the South Platte River."

"The creek of boulders was in the mountains," Eva recollected. "To get there we had traveled down the river they now call the South Platte. I remember at one point, we turned west and traveled into the mountains."

Slowly, the tall man remembered some of the forts. One was Fort Vasquez, and another was Fort Lupton. While they were called forts, they were more like the one Louie was at: A privately owned, walled trading post. The forts along the South Platte would trade with the Arapahoe and Cheyenne for the buffalo hides from their summer hunts.

Tom sat back and looked at his sketch and notes. "If I remember correctly, the trapper I spoke with said the creek was just over a week's travel south."

Eva chuckled. "That I do not remember," she said. "Being young, the trip seemed much longer." She had finished nursing little Isaac and patted his back softly to get him to burp.

Picking up the piece of paper, Tom retrieved his hat from the hook near the door. "I don't want to get your hopes up," he warned Eva. "I am going to talk with Louie. While the money we have is more than I've ever had on me before, it might prove to be far too little to stock a trading post."

"Then we can start small," she said. "You love to build, and there was plenty of timber as I recall. It may start as our cabin with a few things for sale. In time, the business will grow."

Again, Tom felt excitement in his stomach. He loved to create things with his own hands and to do so among the mountain peaks would exceed his wildest dreams. The tall man dashed out the door, and then stopped.

Sticking his head back into the room, he smiled at his family and said, "Wish me luck. I'll be right back."

Eva laid back on the bed with the drowsy baby beside her. She was happy. What Tom hadn't realized was that they would be moving to the creek of boulders to build their future home, a place where she had spent a childhood summer and had never forgotten. They wouldn't need a business to do so. The area offered everything they'd need to survive. It was probably her Arapahoe upbringing that made her confident that the mountains themselves would provide for their needs.

Tom hurried up the trail to the trading post. His mind raced as he thought about how he would present his plan to Louie. As he walked, the mountain man watched as the last of the barricade which had been Fort William hit the ground, raising a cloud of dust. He caught sight of Louie on the porch, witnessing the end.

He turned to the sound of Tom coming up the path. "That's it," the grizzled owner said. "The last of the fort is gone."

"You still have much," Tom pointed out. "There's the saloon, the livery, and your trading post."

"The trading post," he sighed. "Nobody will come here to trade. They will want to go the new fort."

Figuring this was a good opening, Tom began to tell Louie of what he and Eva had been thinking about. The owner led him inside and poured a rye for the two of them. "You and Eva want to start a trading post down on the South Platte?"

"Well, it wouldn't be on the South Platte River," Tom replied. "There is a creek they call the creek of boulders that we would build on."

"So, you want to move away from the trade route and start a trading post," Louie said, sipping on the rye.

"I get the feeling you don't think much of the idea," Tom said. "I was hoping to work something out with you to help stock the post."

"You know that Fort Vasquez went bankrupt, don't you?" the owner asked.

"I hadn't heard that," Tom admitted.

"Fort Jackson went under after just two years down there," Louie added. "You would be going up against Fort Saint Vrain."

Much of the excitement the mountain man had felt was gone. When he and Eva had been talking, it had seemed so simple. Then he heard Louie say, "Fort Lupton is also on the South Platte."

Feeling frustrated, Tom said, a little more sharply than he had intended to, "I understand. There are other trading posts in the area."

Louie poured him another drink. "How much had you planned to invest in the trading post?"

The amount of money Tom had almost made him feel silly as he heard himself say, "We have near $500."

The owner shook his head. "So little." Then he shrugged his shoulders and added, "I had less when I started."

Forcing a smile, Tom said, "I take it Eva and I should forget about it."

"I would never say that," Louie replied. "To build a trading post and stock it, would take $10,000." Seeing the look of defeat on Tom's face he continued, "Of course, a smart man can do it for less. Maybe much less."

"I could get work building the new fort and try and save money," Tom said. "By the time the fort is finished, and with buffalo hunting in the summers, I might have enough to start the trading post."

"Go and talk with Eva," Louie suggested. "I need to do some thinking. Let me know what she says tomorrow."

The mountain man appreciated the gentle way the owner had brushed him off. Tom was sure that

Louie figured Eva would convince him to abandon the idea of a trading post. He found her sitting on the bench looking at the river.

"Did you talked to Louie?" she asked as she handed the baby to him.

While Tom told her about the visit with the grizzled owner, she sat staring at him with little expression. When he was finally done talking she said, "It is settled then. We will leave as soon as I get things packed."

"You don't understand," Tom said, feeling frustrated. "It is not enough money. We have to stay here and work to save more. Maybe in a few years we can go."

"So, you see us living in the cabin, while you work on the fort," Eva said. "In the summer we would hunt buffalo and sell the hides."

When she repeated it, it sounded worse than when Tom had thought it. "Yes, pretty much so."

"Is there no buffalo to the south?" she asked. "Is there no way for us to earn money along the creek of boulders?"

"It would take years to build and start a trading post if we left here now," the mountain man explained.

Eva smiled, "Yes it would, and we'd be doing it together, in the mountains you love."

Suddenly the mountain man felt foolish. He had been so focused on going to the creek of boulders and opening a trading post, that he hadn't even thought about building a home there first. With time, if it worked out, they would have a trading post. It would be just a future goal, not something they were dependent on to make the move.

A broad grin broke out on Tom's bearded face.

"How long will you need to be ready to go?"

The next day, with a spring in his step, the mountain man went back to see Louie. The owner was busy sorting furs brought in by a trapper. Tom poured himself a mug of coffee while watching the two men dicker on the price. Once settled, the trapper began to select items he'd need from the well-stocked shelves.

Louie got himself coffee and came over to join Tom. "What did Eva think?"

"She is packing and planning for the move right now," the tall man said. "We will be going to the cabin to get a few things tomorrow. Then we'll head south and build ourselves a home in the mountains. In time we may have a trading post."

Nodding, Louie looked around his shelves. "It is no secret that I plan to close this place. Right now, I have more stock than I need and I made a deal with the folks at Fort Saint Vrain to purchase some. I'll need someone to bring it to the South Platte."

"If you're looking for someone, Eva and I will be heading that way," Tom said, watching his friend closely.

"They don't want traps," Louie said. "They tend to sell to folks traveling to Santa Fe, or buffalo hunters."

For the next several hours the two men talked, with the result being Tom and Eva would lead a caravan of mules with supplies down to Fort Saint Vrain. Tom would purchase much of the stock that trappers needed for his own use or for a future business. The tall man still had the wagon, and that would be filled with items needed to build his and Eva's cabin. It would include a used nine plate stove.

When they were drinking a toast to the plan,

Louie suddenly slapped his knee. "I got one more thing I been meaning to mention to you."

Surprised at the sudden outburst, Tom asked, "What would that be?"

"A couple of hunters come by here last week looking for a place to spend winters," the owner said. "They mentioned seeing your cabin, but I'd told them it wasn't for sale."

"Well, that has changed," Tom told him.

"It has," Louie replied. "I think they are still around and I see what I can get you for the place."

* * *

It took several days before everything was ready and Tom and Eva returned from the cabin. Going back to the small building on the pond brought back bad memories for both and they were glad to say goodbye to the cabin. Tom was pleased to find that Two Buffalo had returned and offered to drive the wagon. Louie had supplied the mules for the caravan and sold Tom a four-horse team to pull the wagon. Once the supplies were delivered, men at Fort Saint Vrain would return the mules to Fort John, packing buffalo hides.

Two Buffalo led the way as they departed Louie's trading post, driving the heavily loaded wagon with his paint tied to the back. Louie and his sister stood, watching them go, waving and shouting well wishes. Eva was riding the roan with Isaac sitting in front of her. The young boy had become too big for the cradle board that was tucked into the wagon for one of their future children.

Tom followed the wagon, leading a caravan of

ten mules. Also riding with them was Chess Handlin. He had joined them for supper one night at the Buffalo Hide Saloon and had become intrigued with Eva's description of the creek of boulders. Having nothing more important to do at the time, he decided to travel with them and see for himself.

It was the beginning of July and they were three days south of Fort John. The travelers began to see the majestic Rockies to the west. On the plains were buffalo and pronghorn grazing. Colorful wild flowers dotted the grass-covered, rolling hills. Chess pointed to a large herd of wooly bison. "We could be back here in a week and fill the wagon with hides in no time."

Laughing at his excited friend, Tom replied, "If you help me build the first rooms of the cabin, I'll help you fill a wagon with hides. We can sell them at Fort Saint Vrain."

Both Chess and Tom took their turns leading the caravan of mules or driving the wagon. Two Buffalo would disappear into the foothills on his paint and return with meat for supper. Eva would let Isaac play around their camp, trying to get attention from the men while she cooked their meals.

Fort Saint Vrain was a two-story adobe structure. It was located 20 miles from the mountains, at the confluence of South Platte River and a creek having the same name as the fort. Tom was glad to get rid of the daily packing and unpacking of the caravan of mules. Eva's eyes glowed with excitement as she looked at the mountains. They were now less than thirty miles from the meadows that her family had summered in.

Tom, Eva, and Chess spent two nights at the fort, making contacts for future business and learning more about the area. Two Buffalo rode down the Saint Vrain Creek to follow it into the mountains and see the creek of boulders for himself. He would also look for the best trail to bring the wagon in.

While looking over the fort's supplies, Marcellin, one of the St. Vrain brothers, approached the mountain man. "They tell me you plan to settle west of here in the mountains. I must warn you about the Mexicans. Their territory is just to the west and there has been a lot of hostility between them and the United States."

"I will take care not to get them angry at me," Tom replied. "I am thankful that the Comancheros don't range this far north."

"They can be ruthless," the brother said. "We have another trading post south of here that has to deal with them."

"It's my understanding that you trade with the Cheyenne and Arapahoe," the mountain man said. "My wife is Arapahoe, and a friend, Two Buffalo, is Cheyenne."

Smiling, Marcellin replied, "You will do well with them. But the Lakota and Crow raid down this far some times. You must stay watchful."

Tom was about to leave when a surprising question came from the brother. "Are you available to guide hunters?"

"Are you talking about hunting buffalo?"

"Buffalo, elk, and bear." the man replied. "Some come to fish also."

Smiling at another opportunity to make some money, Tom said, "If you get anyone looking for a guide, let me know."

Finally, with the business finished at the fort,

and with Chess driving the wagon, the group rode southwest along the Saint Vrain Creek in search of an area to build their future home. Once they settled on an area, Tom would return to the fort to register the site.

The climb into the mountains was slow and they had to rest the team several times. They were following a trail used by trappers in the heyday of beaver. Two Buffalo spoke of a valley that he had found that would be protected from winter storms coming in from the northwest. It offered grazing for the animals and timber to build. To the west were several ponds and lakes.

Eva kept pointing to features that reminded her of her childhood trip. Late in the afternoon, they pulled into the valley that the chief had spoken of. Eva squealed with delight as she looked around.

"This may not have been the valley that we summered in," she said, "but it looks every bit like the one father brought us to."

Helping her and Isaac off the roan, she and Tom looked at the mountains rising to the northwest. Directly west, they would have a view of the sun setting over the distant Rockies. Taking her into his arms, the mountain man whispered, "Welcome home, Eva."

NOTES

Made in United States
Cleveland, OH
21 July 2025